A CANDLELIGHT ROMANCE

CANDLELIGHT ROMANCES

LOVE
IN THE
WILDS

Suzanne Roberts

A CANDLELIGHT ROMANCE

Published by
Dell Publishing Co., Inc.
1 Dag Hammarskjold Plaza
New York, New York 10017

Dell ® TM 681510, Dell Publishing Co., Inc.

ISBN: 0-440-14837-5

Printed in the United States of America

First printing—August 1980

ONE

The land had a dreamlike improbability about it; there seemed to be an ocean of grass, grass of a peculiar light green, the color of shallow tropic seas. It appeared to be endless in expanse, flecked everywhere with the fleeing figures of wild animals—thousands upon uncountable, incredible thousands. Beyond this there were low mountains, rocky outcrops like strange ships sailing a flat, inland sea.

Jennifer, peering out the window of the plane, could see zebras and gazelles grazing, while vultures flew above them in an effortless circle beneath the descending plane. The sky around them was serene and blue; now, she could make out the air terminal at Nairobi, a low, whitewashed building with palm trees all around it.

The plane came to a smooth landing and people began unfastening seatbelts, gathering up belongings, saying goodbye to each other. It had taken three jets to get her here; she had lost track of the hours, due to long layovers in Morocco and Gabon. She had been tired, very tired, as she left New York to begin the first long leg of the trip, but now, she suddenly felt renewed, uplifted, and a growing sense of excitement began in her.

She had not anticipated the heat; it came upon her like a moist steambath, taking her breath for a second, making her feel dizzy. Then, with the others, she made her way down the steps of the big plane and walked across the expanse of cement glistening in the brilliant sunlight. She must look for Maggie; she should have wired from Morocco—the plane was terribly late—

"Jennifer? Jennifer Logan?"

Jenny turned quickly around. The woman was smiling,

7

in her late fifties, perhaps, with friendly blue eyes peering over large sunglasses. She wore a white floppy hat and pants suit; she looked rather like one of the well-to-do ladies from New England, in town for a day's shopping.

"Aunt Margaret?"

"So," the older woman said, beginning to smile. "It is you! Yes; I should have known—I remember your eyes." She hugged Jennifer; there was the pleasant, cool scent of cologne. "I expect you're dead on your feet, poor darling. I've been hanging around here half the day, waiting for you."

They were walking through the terminal. It was large, not so big as those in New York, but very modern. People embraced each other, talking in a language Jenny didn't understand, but, unlike when she was in Morocco, she was certain it wasn't French.

"I'm terribly sorry," she said, allowing herself to be guided toward the baggage department. "The plane had some sort of mechanical problem and we had to wait for hours."

"Well, at least you're here, my dear, safe and sound." The brilliant blue eyes glanced at her again. "Are you all right? Perhaps you'd like a cool drink before we go to the reserve."

"That would be nice."

"Good. Go on in and order something—get a sandwich too, because my cook won't be in until morning; she's gone to help her daughter have a baby. I'll see to your baggage and get them in the jeep—you just go on in and find a table."

Jenny nodded and obediently went into a large, very pleasantly cool room where food and drinks were being served by white-coated waiters. She should have realized that her great-aunt would be very efficient; Maggie had raised Jenny's mother and her mother had been like that. She blinked her eyes in the near-darkness of the room and

8

finally made her way to a window table with shaded green glass. From this vantage point, she could see the brown mountains and the waves of pale green grass beyond the airport.

Well, she'd done it. Made the decision, turned her life around, headed in a new and, she hoped, far better direction. A smiling waiter appeared almost instantly with a pitcher of fresh iced tea, poured a glass for Jennifer, and inquired in nearly perfect English about her order.

"Someone else is coming, thank you. I believe we're going to have a sandwich."

It surprised her a little that the menu, printed in three languages, contained things that were familiar—eggs, salads, fresh fruits in season, cold chicken. Perhaps it wouldn't all seem so strange after all. Perhaps she would be able to adjust at once, finding that the stories she'd heard of Africa—tales of dark places, weird voodoo rites, vicious animals, and poison darts—were all foolish.

Perhaps in no time at all, she would be able to erase every memory of Brendon Miles and the mistake she had very nearly made with him. She had managed, on the long, arduous flight over, not to think of the life she was leaving behind her—her job at the advertising agency, her nice little apartment she'd waited nearly a year and a half to get, the pulsing, exciting pace of New York. But now, sitting there waiting for her great-aunt, the dreaded feelings— feelings that asked what on earth was she doing here, why had she made such a decision in such a brief time, was it too late to make a transatlantic call and get it all back again—began to come to her.

The surprising letter from Maggie had come just two weeks ago, with a warm invitation to come and spend some time in Africa "any time you please." Jennifer, who had spent many sleepless nights trying to make up her mind about Brendon Miles, had seen the letter as some sort of enchanted, heaven-sent messenger, offering her a quick way out of her problems. Staying in New York meant working for Brendon; it seemed unthinkable to quit, to go to work in some other place, have another boss, live in the same city as he did and never see him again. She had felt trapped, doomed, locked in a snowballing situation that drew her nearer and nearer to a sexual affair with him, an affair she did not really want.

Now, she was safe, safe from that, at least. She might miss her life, her job, her apartment, miss seeing him—but at least, she wouldn't end up like so many young girls—involved in a heartbreaking affair with her married boss.

Maggie hurried into the room, glanced around, and, seeing Jennifer, came over to the table, taking off her wide-brimmed hat. Her hair, like Jennifer's, was rich, dark auburn, without a trace of gray in it. There were fine lines around and under Maggie's blue eyes, however, but still, she seemed young and full of energy. It had been seven years since Jennifer had seen her last; Maggie and her husband had flown over for the sad funeral of Jenny's mother. Since that time, Maggie's husband had died—Jenny had sent a cable at the time, and now, she realized it seemed odd to see her aunt without Jack. They had been married nearly forty years when he died of a poison arrow meant for a leopard.

"I've had your luggage loaded in the jeep," her aunt said, sipping the cold tea. "You didn't bring much, did you? That was very clever of you."

"I'm afraid I left in rather a hurry." No need to tell all of it, not just now. If her aunt could recover so beautifully from losing her beloved husband, surely she, Jennifer, could quickly get over a man she shouldn't ever have wanted in the first place!

"I really didn't expect you to come, you know," Maggie said, her eyes studying Jennifer. She smiled, her hand reaching out for Jenny's. "But I'm awfully glad you did. Frankly, I've had my bad moments since I lost Jack. No," she said quickly, "please don't sympathize. We had thirty-nine perfect years together and I'll be darned if I'm going to give in to self-pity. Some women never find what I had with him."

"Some of us get sidetracked," Jenny said, and she saw something spark in her aunt's blue eyes, some kind of intelligent, quick reasoning. Surely she must have wondered at Jenny's quick decision to quit her job and come here, with only a brief cable to announce the time of her arrival.

Maggie patted her hand, then turned her attention to the menu.

"Try the cold chicken, dear; it's probably very good here. After today, you can start acquiring a taste for authentic African food."

"I'm sure I will."

"First we'll have our lunch, then, when I've got you back at the house, and rested, we can talk. If you feel like it, that is."

So she did suspect there was a reason for the hasty exit, the retreat from New York, the strange turnabout and the cable, asking if Jenny might come to Kenya and stay "forever, maybe, if you could help me find a job, Aunt Margaret. . . ."

It was a powerful-sounding motor under the hood of that oversized, four-wheel-drive vehicle, and Maggie handled it as if she'd been born to it. In what seemed like no time at all they were on their way, breezing down the modern highway and finally, turning off on a narrow road that led to the bush country. Here, only five miles outside the city, Jennifer was introduced to the cold, unchanging Africa. They were passing a hunting camp; dusty and seemingly deserted, a glinting mound of wire snares seemed to be everywhere, on both sides of the road. Jennifer, wearing a large-brimmed, borrowed hat (Maggie had thoughtfully brought one along) looked at them without understanding.

11

"Damn!" It was Maggie, her mouth grim. "No matter how many game scouts tear those obscene, evil things down, the poachers always put them back up again!"

"What on earth are they?" Jenny had to nearly shout above the roar of the engine. "What are they for?"

"To kill, that's what." Maggie's tanned face was expressionless, but there was deep contempt in her voice. "Death by snare. Vicious, slow torture. The animal catches its neck or leg in a loop and tries to escape—the harder it pulls, the deeper the noose sinks into its flesh. I've seen some of them with their heads nearly torn off from the snares, or legs missing."

"But—how can—why do they allow—" A kind of slow horror was washing over Jenny. She had not bargained on cruelty, although of course, she should have expected it, in one form or another, in this still-primitive country.

"Oh, they're outlawed," Maggie said above the noise of the motor, "but that doesn't stop them. Some of them, the poachers, work for commercial syndicates. It isn't going to end until stupid, vain women stop buying coats made of skins, or handbags made of crocodile—even some perfumes have aphrodisiacs made out of pulverized rhino horn. Looks like we'll have to do another big sweep, and get all the snares we can. But they'll be back in a week or two. They always are."

"And you—the government, can't stop them?"

"Not for long. Poachers usually believe they have a God-given right to kill the game." Maggie glanced at Jennifer. "Sit tight now, we're coming to a sharp turn." She twisted the steering wheel as Jenny held her breath. They were going up a steep hill; to the right and left of them the pale grass flowed like a shimmering green curtain. "*Nyama ya mungu*," Maggie said.

The road narrowed; Jenny put both hands on the seat and clutched it.

"What did you say?"

"That's a Swahili phrase which means 'meat of God.' The poachers think they have a divine right. Don't worry, you won't tumble out. I've never lost a passenger yet from this old crate!" Maggie shifted into high gear as they climbed the steep hill. "I've only got one rule about riding in this machine and that's that I don't drive at night anymore, because of the arrows."

"Did you say arrows?" Jennifer's voice was alarmed.

"In very thick bush, you can't see very well, so you can't duck. We're coming into that sort of terrain just now. The bloody poachers use them, of course, to kill game—the arrows are poisoned and when the poison is fresh, it'll kill a wild animal in thirty minutes." She stared straight ahead. "Jack died on our front porch. He'd managed to drive the jeep to the reserve and on to our house there, but there wasn't even time to call a doctor. It was dark, you see—he was just on his way home from Nairobi. I never go out at night anymore; it's the one rule I must insist you obey, Jenny."

Jenny nodded, still clutching the seat. Was she, she wondered, going to be afraid, always afraid of something terrible happening while she was here? She stared at the brilliant green grass as they drove onward. It might be good for her to feel fear, to worry about things like wire snares and poison arrows; fear might be a kind of purging for her, a release from a very different kind of trap—the one she'd nearly fallen into because of Brendon Miles.

They entered the reserve shortly before dusk. The large wooden gate was lifted to let the jeep pass through by a smiling black child who grinned in delight as Maggie handed him a small bag of candy bought in Nairobi.

"That's Massukuntna's grandson," she told Jenny. "You'll meet Massukuntna at the house, most likely. His wife is my cook, but as I told you, she's away until morning."

The old man, a tall, spare Shangaan elder, was waiting

for them, squatting on the wide porch of the main house, smoking a long pipe. He stood up as Maggie pulled up, parking the jeep.

"He'll bring your things, Jenny." She waved as the old man approached them.

"No rain yet," he said, his eyes watching Jennifer, the newcomer. "Rain won't come for another two weeks. I had a dream that told me."

"Well, you haven't been wrong yet, Massukuntna. This is Jennifer Logan, my great-niece, child of my sister's daughter."

Jenny, suddenly feeling a bit shy, put out a friendly hand, but the old man didn't take it. Instead, he made a rather formal bow and began unloading her suitcases.

"We'll have a drink on the porch if you like," Maggie said. She led the way to the wide, screened door, and held it open. "It usually takes people around here a while to get friendly, but when they do, they love you for life. So don't be offended."

"I'm not."

They were inside the house, in the hallway. It was blessedly cool; fans from the inner rooms caught the air and sent it wafting throughout the entire, shaded house. Jennifer, following her aunt up the lovely, carved staircase, began to think of a cooling bath and the first solid night's rest she'd had since getting Maggie's invitation.

"Jack and I always called this the guest room," Maggie said, pushing open one of the bedroom doors. "Now, it can be your room, for as long as you want to stay." She was busy opening the windows, the deep closet, turning down the white-sheeted, double brass bed. Suddenly, her face was serious. "After you let me know you were coming, I told myself I ought to write to you or cable you or something— and tell you something about what you could expect. But I had the feeling that you were very anxious to get away from New York."

"Yes," Jenny said quietly, "I was."

The old man had brought the bags, setting them down just outside the door. Once again, he looked hard at Jenny, his eyes appraising and intelligent.

"Then it's good you came," Maggie said, "even though this place takes some getting used to."

That, Jenny was to learn, was putting it mildly. The big house had ten rooms, not including the spacious kitchen, and a porch that faced Lake Naivasha. Beyond, in the back, was the deep green forest and brush, and to the west lay the rain forest. The house was elevated somewhat, with the porch resting on imbedded poles, so that there was altogether a stunning view of the blue lake and the lush vegetation. Left alone in her bedroom, Jenny, wearing her bathrobe, leaned out the window and called to Maggie, who sat on the front porch, feet propped up on the porch railing.

"Aunt Maggie?"

Maggie put down her drink and squinted upward in the fading sunlight.

"I guess you found out, Jenny." She was close to smiling.

"I can't find—there doesn't seem to be—"

"A bathtub?"

"Yes."

"Come on down and have your shower, dear."

"Down? Down there?" Jenny stared in surprise at the odd-looking contraption her aunt was pointing to. It was a sort of round, fenced-in structure with a cloth bag suspended overhead by rather frayed-looking ropes. "You mean I'm supposed to shower out there—in the *yard*?"

"Water's all ready for you, dear, nice and warm. You'll find some lovely French soap in the top drawer of the bureau. Bring a towel, dear, and shampoo—it's French too—I have it sent from the Ivory Coast." She grinned, finally. "Taking an outdoor shower always surprises my guests from the States, but you'll get used to it."

At first, Jenny felt ill-at-ease about taking off her robe, standing nude inside that rustic-fence enclosure, but then she realized the fence actually came up to her chin, or nearly so, and the only living things rude enough to stare were six or so monkeys who sat or lounged in a big tree nearby. Every time Jenny pulled the rope to pour warm water on herself, the creatures made a strange, screaming noise and a few of them, Jenny noted with amazement, even clapped their little hands.

Whether it was the hard-milled soap, the rich shampoo in the pretty bottle, or perhaps wildflowers growing nearby, she didn't know, but there was a lovely fragrance wafting around her as she showered, and the water was as soft as milk, flowing over her slender body. She began to feel better, much, much better, and finally, after rinsing her freshly washed, shoulder-length hair, she found herself laughing out loud at the antics of the little monkeys. One of them, flirting with her, showing off, swung from tree to nearby tree, scolding and chattering, turning his tiny, hairy head to see if Jenny was watching.

She toweled herself dry and, wrapping the soft towel around her head, got into her robe and stepped outside the confines of the makeshift shower. She looked toward the porch, but her aunt must have gone inside. The whole house seemed to glow with a soft light—candles—and it occurred to Jenny that there probably wasn't any electricity here at all. *Good*, she told herself, walking through the deepening shadows towards the house, *no lights, no phone, no radio or television—wonderful!* The world she had come from would surely dissolve into a kind of muted background, which was exactly what she wanted it to do!

Aunt Maggie said nothing that night to Jenny, nothing about why she had come so suddenly, and as the two women said goodnight an hour or so after Jenny's lovely shower, she still had asked no real questions. There would, thank God, be plenty of time for talk. Perhaps, Jenny thought, a good, honest talk with a kind and understanding woman was exactly what she needed; she had not spoken to anyone about her near-affair with Brendon, not even the other girls in the office, although she felt quite certain that they knew.

Her boss, at forty, had been attractive, there was no mistake about that. Stunned with grief at the sudden death of her youngish mother, Jennifer moved from the somewhat staid little town in Maryland to New York—and was almost instantly swept up in an atmosphere of intrigue and romance.

Perhaps, she was to realize much later, she had been looking for something, someone, to love, and unfortunately, Brendon had made himself all too available. What began with a kind of light bantering in the office developed into his inviting her to attend television shows with him ("Make lots of notes," he told her, and she believed him) because many of their advertising clients had spots on TV. After that, it seemed only natural to allow her kind boss to buy her a very late supper, after a show's taping, and drive her to her small, East-side apartment.

How could she have been so naive, so foolish? By the time he finally got around to kissing her, in his car, outside her apartment, she imagined herself to be in love with him. After that, she refused to attend the show tapings, refused the suppers, even the phone calls he'd make from a bar someplace in Manhattan. She had the usual symptoms— the burning desire to see what his wife looked like, the insane eagerness to believe his wife really was the wicked witch Brendon said she was, the dreams about making love, the conflict about wanting to quit her job and being afraid she'd be sorry—

But now, lying in that big, soft bed with the netting over it, with the silvery moonlight making blue-white puddles on the scrubbed wood floor, all of that seemed misty and almost dim to her, as if she had really put it away forever. Or as if it had not really been important and was very easily forgotten.

She slept a dreamless, exhausted sleep, finally opening her eyes at some sound. For a second, she did not know where she was; the room was silent, still bathed in the blue and silver light, and a moist breeze, forerunner of the monsoon season due anytime, cooled the large bedroom. Jenny turned her head to look at the small traveling clock she'd remembered to bring along: quarter past two. She had been in bed and asleep since before ten.

The sound she heard was music. She listened, not at all sure that she wasn't dreaming, and deciding she wasn't, got out of bed, pushing back the clean-smelling mosquito netting to go to the open window. Then, she put her ear against the sturdy screen and listened once again.

It was definitely music, very raucous, the blaring, disco beat she'd learned to hate in New York. There had been lots of dates at the end of her stay there, men who took her dancing, young men who were supposed to erase her threatening feelings for Brendon Miles, but didn't. She had gotten mightily sick of that kind of music, and now, it came as a mild shock to hear it of all places, here, in this remote and peaceful place in Africa. Drums, native drums, wouldn't have surprised her; they would have been pleasing to hear, in fact, but this music—where could it be coming from?

It seemed to come and go, drifting in on the night wind, so she speculated that wherever it was, it was very likely some distance away. Finally, she crawled back into the comfortable bed, closed her eyes and once again, slept.

She awoke to a discreet tapping at the door, then a plump, smiling black woman came in.

"Good morning. I am Manguana; your aunt usually has her tea downstairs, but if you like, I can bring you a cup here, although I'm very busy with the children this morning."

18

"Oh no," Jenny said quickly; she wasn't used to the idea of having anyone do anything for her. "I'll get a cup myself, thank you, in the kitchen." She realized she had slept very well and felt surprisingly good, refreshed. "Aunt Maggie told me you were helping deliver a baby yesterday."

Manguana smiled. "A boy, very fat and handsome." She was, Jenny realized, quite old, and yet, her skin was satin-smooth and nearly unwrinkled. "I'll make you a nice honey cake for your second tea today. Massukuntna told me you are far too skinny."

"Massukuntna? Oh yes—your husband." Jenny smiled. "That would be lovely, thank you."

In the bathroom, Jenny took a good long look at herself in the old-fashioned, full-length mirror. Yes; she was a bit too thin, but thin in New York had somehow meant something different from what it apparently did here. In New York, she had always felt a certain pressure, as if she had been asked to run someplace, hurry up and run someplace. How long had it been since she'd really felt at ease with herself, with life, so that she could enjoy just sleeping or eating?

Too long. She stepped out of her nightgown and stretched, beginning to feel a lovely sense of anticipation. Her amber-colored hair and matching eyes were like her mother's, Laura's, but Jenny had never felt beautiful. It was her mother who had attracted men; they had sought her, loved her, wanted her—and she had married and divorced three of them before her death.

She found Maggie sitting on the porch behind a small table, typing, her glasses slightly down on her nose.

"There you are, Jenny. I hope you rested well—you look as if you took a magic beauty pill. I'd forgotten what lovely hair we Kenton women have. Red but not brassy. I see you've got a cup; have more tea, dear."

Jenny settled herself in a comfortable wicker rocker that faced the lake.

19

"Kenton women?"

"That was Mama's maiden name, dear. Your great-grand-mother's too, of course. We've all got her hair, God rest her restless soul. Are you feeling better?"

"Much better, thank you. Manguana said she'll make me a honey cake. She thinks I'm far too skinny."

Maggie laughed, taking off her glasses. "She told me that, too, when I first came here with Jack. That was twenty-five years ago, when your mother married your father and I felt I could do as I pleased at last. Jack so wanted to take this job here—so off we came." She gazed out at the lake. "I've asked myself a thousand times if I'd do it over, if I'd come here again, knowing I'd lose him the way I did."

There was a small silence. "Would you, Aunt Maggie?" Jenny's voice was gentle. She had always been fascinated by love, the blinding, spellbinding love that sometimes happened between a man and a woman. She had seen her mother in love, or what passed for love, but it never had lasted. Her mother had always tired of men, always had wanted out of the arrangement, finally. But Maggie—what Maggie and her man once had was very real and beautiful; Jenny could believe that because even now, her aunt's eyes shone when she spoke of the years with him.

"I'm not really sure, Jenny. He was happy here; he loved Africa and the people here—but mostly, I'd give anything to do it over again, do it all over and refuse to come here. I'd somehow convince him to keep on with his veter-inary practice in Maryland. I guess," she said, going back to her typing, "that only happens at night. One gets a bit weary of sleeping in a half-warmed bed, you know." She looked at Jenny as if to dispel the sudden mood of gloom. "Look, why don't you type this for me, dear? I've always been rotten at typing, I'm afraid. I've written a letter to our office in Nairobi about the poachers' traps we saw coming down here, requesting they sweep the snares."

"I'd love to," Jenny told her. She took her aunt's place at

20

the small typewriting table. "Oh, by the way, Aunt Maggie, I heard music last night, coming from the south, I think it was. What on earth was that?"

Instantly, Maggie's tanned face seemed to go pale; her blue eyes flashed what could only have been outrage.

"Music? This far away? Damn him—that man has no decency at all! There was Manguana's daughter, having her baby in the village, and I'll bet that music was even louder there! And the animals—anything could disturb them, make them upset or nervous—"

"But where was it coming from?"

Maggie, her mouth showing her anger, had opened a desk drawer and was holding a powerful-looking pair of binoculars up to her eyes. "From the lodge, my dear. From Damien Lear's infamous hunting lodge. One would think that when those rich idiots he lets stay there go off on their safaris, they'd want to get a good night's rest before doing their killing. But no—they're up at all hours, carousing and drinking and listening to that insane music!"

Jenny wisely asked no more questions about the mysterious Damien Lear that morning. Whoever, whatever, he was, Maggie very clearly despised him—and Jenny had never before seen her good-natured aunt dislike anybody!

The letter typing, along with a somewhat detailed report containing figures on the past month's budget for the reserve, took up all of the morning. Jenny took a moment to have more tea, along with Manguana's delicious honey cake (warm, sweet, filled with peanuts and thick honey), then she stood up, stretched, and walked with Maggie to the shelter house built for the monkeys.

"We fence in all the animals we can," Maggie told her as she strung up golden, ripe bananas onto a hanging rope. "The monkeys, of course, we can't very well contain. They come into the reserve, eat, chatter, look around and then go back to the bush, most of them. Some of them stay, though—like old Lovely here." She reached up and

21

handed a banana to a bright-eyed little monkey who'd been watching them from her vantage point on a giant tree limb.

"Lovely?"

Maggie smiled. "It seemed like a proper name for her, since she's so sweet-natured. When you've been here awhile, Jenny, you'll find yourself changing your ideas about animals. You won't find a single one of them repulsive or ugly. It may amaze you to know that one actually comes to revere them, because they, like us, are God's, aren't they?"

The two women worked side by side, stringing the fruit onto the rope, pouring fresh lake water they carried in buckets into the watering troughs, putting fresh straw down for one very pregnant monkey who seemed content to sit and chew on grass instead of eating with the others.

"Aunt Maggie," Jenny asked finally, as they walked back toward the house together, "do you mind telling me why you dislike that man so?"

There was a small silence; only a tightening of Maggie's jaw told of her reaction to the name.

"He's a killer," she said finally, as they came in sight of the house. "That's why."

"A killer! I don't understand—"

"Jack didn't agree with me, but my husband was a saint and I'm not. We both knew Damien Lear from the time he first came here, and we knew when he bought that piece of land that it was to be used for the wrong purpose."

"For what purpose?"

"Money. Drinking and getting up at dawn to stumble out and kill animals. That's what those paying guests of his do, most of them. Not only that, he thinks we're all a bunch of bleeding hearts here at the reserve, that it goes against nature to look out for wild animals, protect them, the way we do. If you want to know what I think, Jenny, I think he's a totally embittered, horrible man who doesn't give a damn about anything—man or animal!"

22

"He sounds terrible," Jenny admitted. "I'm sorry if I got you all upset."

"I mean to send a note over there," Maggie muttered. "I'm going to let him know that if he doesn't turn down his bloody taped music, I see to it that a curse is put on him!"

"A curse! Aunt Maggie, you don't actually believe in that sort of thing, do you?"

"No, and neither does he. But at least," her aunt said as they climbed the porch steps, "he'll know how riled up I am!"

There were children living on the reserve grounds with their parents, some twenty little ones in all. While their parents worked on the reserve, they usually played around the main house. This time they accompanied Jenny while she fed the animals and they napped while she spent the remainder of the day doing some bookkeeping chores for Maggie. At dusk, Jenny walked alone to the lake to watch a pack of cheetahs drink and nurse their young.

There was a feeling of peace beginning to filter into her, a sort of lovely magic that filled her with a sense of energy yet allowed her to sit content in absolute stillness as she watched the rain forest birds and animals at close range.

Even the oppressive heat this evening didn't change her happy mood.

"Things will be released when the rains come," Maggie said, sipping a glass of white wine with her soup. "When the time for the rain gets near like this, things get—pent up. It always happens." She looked at Jenny over the candlelight. Manguana had set a card table up for them, on the porch, with candles and wine Maggie said she'd been saving for company.

"I don't want to be that," Jenny told her. "I don't want to be company."

"Be whatever makes you feel best, my dear."

"What I'm trying to say is—Aunt Maggie—you told me I could stay on if I wanted to. Did you really mean that?"

"Of course. But I think it's far too soon for you to make up your mind to that. When the time is right, I'll take you on a bush tour. I want you to see a bit of what Damien Lear tries so hard to keep as it is. But you aren't ready for that sort of horror yet. We'll go before the rains come."

Slowly, Jenny put down her spoon. The soup was very filling, with herring and some sort of sweet-tasting meat and okra and eggs in it. She was used to eating very little.

"Horror?"

Maggie nodded. "Yes, horror. And Damien says it's survival of the fittest. Some of them die miserably. Last week we found a female waterbuck who'd gone to the lake to drink, full of fever. He claims that what we're doing here is nothing but zookeeping. But as I said, he's an angry, bitter man, in spite of what he pretends to be." She put down her wine glass. "I'm going to bed, Jennifer. No more of this morbid talk, if you don't mind. Speaking of Damien Lear this late in the day might very well give me nightmares!" She leaned over and gently kissed Jenny's smooth cheek. "Sleep well."

"Goodnight, Aunt Maggie."

But this night, Jenny could not sleep no matter how hard she tried. Finally, she realized that *trying* to sleep was foolish, so she put on her robe and padded barefoot down the freshly scrubbed wooden stairs and out to the porch.

The night sky was stunningly beautiful, filled with gray and silver rain clouds, rolling, boiling, moving across the high face of the moon, seeming to change color from silver to purple and blue, coming lower and lower, like some mysterious, mystical bag filled with endless water about to dump itself on the dry forest. She understood that feeling of release her aunt had talked about, the sudden feeling of freedom when the rains finally came.

And as she watched that silver-streaked sky, they began, the slow droplets of water. At first, Jenny thought it was only some night bug on the leaves of the orchids that grew wild all around the porch, but then another came, and another, making a little sound, a quick, steady little tune. A bird screamed from somewhere in the rain forest nearby, flying swiftly toward the clouds, as if it couldn't wait for the blessed, cooling water to fall upon it but must go and meet it on its way down.

Jenny stepped from the high porch to the yard as if she were in a trance; Massukuntna had been wrong this time, mistaken this time, for he had said it would come in two weeks. But here it was; here it came, heavier now, beginning with an earnestness that soaked her hair and her thin nightgown and made cool mud of the dirt under her bare feet. She stood in the yard with her face upraised, loving the feel of its softness on her face, on her body, like a lover's caress—soothing and yet exciting . . .

A new time had begun then, in this part of the world. A time of renewal, of strength, a time when the weary trees and thirsty lakes could replenish themselves. From their shelter house, the monkeys screeched out in excitement and beyond, in the rain forest, she could see the great trees moving as animals moved in them with a sense of joy and urgency.

Suddenly, a window opened and Maggie's scolding voice called to Jenny:

"Jennifer! Do you want to get the chills?"

Jenny took a deep breath. "All right—I'm coming in!"

But on the porch step, she turned to listen. There was no music coming from Damien Lear's lodge tonight. Either he had taken Maggie's message seriously or else even such a man as he was enchanted by the unexpected flow from the skies, coming so much sooner than expected.

And surely, Jenny thought, smiling her thanks as her aunt put a huge dry towel around her shoulders, surely that was a very good sign, this early rain, as if, like the thirsty trees in the forest, she too could be renewed, changed, given new joy and strength!

TWO

No matter how early in the morning Jennifer got up, dressed, quickly washed up and hurried downstairs, her aunt was always already there, calmly sitting at her desk in the study, usually with a finished tea tray nearby.

"Good morning," Maggie would say sweetly, "did you oversleep this morning, dear?"

Usually, it would barely be light outside. And now that the rainy season had come, it was darkish all day long, but that didn't mean the chores lessened in any way. On the contrary, there seemed to be more to do now than ever, since keeping the young animals dry was very important.

There was, as Maggie said, so much to lose, so much to save, by helping them. Within that first week there, Jennifer had watched in awe as a lioness, regal, haughty, usually amused-looking when tourists were frightened of her, give birth to three fat cubs. The following day, a baby elephant was born and promptly named Peanuts by Jenny and the children who usually went with her when she did the feeding.

So gradually, she was unwinding, getting used to and actually becoming a part of this strange, secluded life. Some people, but not all of them on the reserve, spoke English, so sign language or a friendly smile or gesture in some cases served to make new friends for Jenny. The children took to her at once and after the feedings outside, she began teaching them little games to play indoors. They taught her games too; she found herself laughing once again.

Afternoons were spent typing for Maggie—reports were endless, copied in triplicate always, sent to parks and other reserves, with bills for food, accounts of money spent, pa-

26

pers to government officials for their stamp of approval, letters to park directors, scientists, veterinarians, rangers, game scouts. She wrote up documented complaints concerning poachers and sent notes to tribal elders from the bush country, asking them to tea.

It was on the day of such an anticipated visit from an elder that Jenny had tea on the screened-in porch. Maggie, with the visiting elder, had gone off to attend to the repairing of a fence knocked down by an angry cheetah, a spoiled old female who had wandered onto the reserve several months before, bleeding badly from the cruelty of a poacher; her tail had been cut off, to be sold and used as a fly whisk.

"Manguana, I haven't heard that music coming from Mr. Lear's lodge lately."

"Your auntie put a stop to it," Manguana said. "Damien Lear sent a letter of apology, but your auntie tore it up."

Manguana, Jenny knew, had worked here with her aunt since both women were relatively young; they were as close as sisters. So whenever Manguana spoke of her Aunt Maggie, Jenny listened. The words, though sometimes harsh-sounding, were always laced with love and affection.

"Tore it up? That isn't like her to do that."

"She gets angry too quickly, sometimes. I expect it comes from missing her man. When he died, she acted like he'd only gone to town and he'd be coming back for supper. But at night, we used to hear her cry. Sometimes we still can hear her." She suddenly looked sad as she rolled raisin dough out for bread. "Dr. Lear is a good man but your auntie doesn't think so." She spoke with a very slight French accent.

"*Dr.* Lear! You don't mean he's actually a medical doctor?"

Manguana nodded. "He doesn't practice anymore." She seemed to want to change the subject. "You should go over to his lodge, maybe make some friends. You'll get lonely here, with the old women and little children and animals. Over there, you could drink a little red wine, dance to some music—"

Jennifer smiled. "No, thank you; I had all the partying and dancing I want, in New York. I've been very happy here, honestly." She put a fresh sheet of paper in the typewriter. For some reason, in spite of meaning what she'd said about feeling happy here, there was a certain feeling of curiosity in her that had been scratched by Manguana's words. "I might stop by the lodge sometime, if it wouldn't offend my aunt." She bent her head to her work. "And Manguana—"

"Yes?"

"You are not old! And neither is my aunt."

A quick smile. "Old enough to have pains when the rains come."

Jenny resumed her work, losing herself in the letters composed in longhand by Maggie, who did not like to type and seemed glad to have Jennifer to do it for her. The current batch of letters contained a heated complaint to officials concerning the finding of a young bushbuck; its foot and leg had been caught in two snare traps. After surgery, the animal limped about the compound, accepting hunks of coarse brown sugar from the children, but, as the letter stated, he would never be able to survive outside the reserve.

Late that afternoon, Maggie left in the jeep with the elder to visit his village and take gifts. He had come laden with gifts for everybody, baskets of exotic herbs for cooking, some beautiful, sturdy pottery, a shawl for Maggie.

The big house was unusually quiet; Jenny took a rain shower (no need for the bucket to dump on one's head), standing a long time in the silky, warm rainwater, soaping all over, finally going back into the house to dress in jeans and a fresh white blouse. She tied her long hair back in a silk scarf, remembering how she had bought it one day on her lunch hour while still in New York, half-planning to wear it sailing with her boss. She hadn't gone on that trip, and the scarf had been one of the few things she'd hurriedly packed to bring.

The usual cluster of children played quietly on the porch, waiting for time to go with Jenny on her daily visit to see the newborn animals in the compound.

"Can you carry a bucket all by yourself, Mieka?" Jenny asked, pantomiming the action.

The little boy nodded, his beautiful dark eyes full of delight. He spoke no English, but he and Jenny had liked each other instantly.

"Okay, then, off we go, children, and kindly button up your raincoats!"

They were all very proud of the new plastic raincoats Maggie had brought them from one of her shopping jaunts to Nairobi, although some of them looked lost inside the long sleeves and ground-length coats. They stood waiting patiently for Jenny while she filled their little buckets with goodies for the reserve's animal babies, sugar and bits of leftover cake and honey bread and three full buckets of sweet, syrupy water with special vitamins stirred in.

"Mustn't eat the sugar, Tania; Mieka dear, please be careful and don't spill!"

So off they all went, walking bravely in the heavy rain, stopping to admire the new baby eland, waiting while Jenny propped a board against a leap-proof fence and made a note to see that it got mended properly. The next step was a large, tin can-constructed cage where a lioness was protected for the time being from her mate while she nursed her new cubs. Jenny and the children stayed their distance, pushing a bucket quickly through the door, then closing it.

She felt somewhat surprised at her own new courage around the wild animals, but as Maggie had told her—

sometimes one found it far easier to deal with animals in their jungle than to deal with humans in theirs!

"Miss Jenny! *Miss Jenny!*"

Jennifer, who had been taking pictures of the new lion cubs, straightened up and peered through the rain as three of the children came running toward her. One of them, the smallest, tripped on his long raincoat and sprawled in the mud. Jenny hurried over to him and helped him up.

"Mozam—are you hurt?" He was crying loudly. "Mozam, what is it?"

She looked helplessly at the other three children who'd gone with him, carrying their buckets, to feed the monkeys. Their eyes were round, and suddenly, two of them began crying, along with little Mozam.

"Did—is one of the baby monkeys sick?"

The rain seemed to come down harder, drenching Jenny and the children. The older ones, the ones who spoke English as well as French and their own language, were not with her; they'd gone with Maggie and the elder.

"Did one of the animals frighten you, honey?"

Unable to understand her, the little boy stuck both little fists into his eyes and cried harder. Jenny gathered him to her; she begun to feel not only mystified but helpless as well.

"Did—did one of the baby monkeys—" It was no use; none of them spoke English, except to be able to say Jenny's name. Besides, they were all crying now, even the bigger ones.

"Go back to the house," she told them, pointing. "Leave your buckets here, children, and go back to Missy Maggie's house, understand?" She gave the tallest of them a gentle shove toward the house, wiped off little Mozam's face with the scarf she'd taken from her hair, and, leaving her own full bucket of sweet milk behind with the others, headed for the large monkey shelter.

The animals there gave out a cheerful series of cries

when they saw her; most of them began showing off immediately, pushing at each other, pretending to snarl, and rolling around in mock fights. Jenny peered inside the shelter, where it was newly swept and clean, smelling of warm hay. She could see the new mother in there, holding her tiny baby. The baby was very much alive; his beady black eyes blinked as Jenny opened the little door, and he tightened his grip on his mother's neck.

Nothing wrong here. Maybe the children had some sort of private quarrel, something to do with the sugar. She very nearly went back to get them, but as she started to, she heard a strange, hair-raising sound coming from the nearby bush, a kind of hoarse keening sound that sounded almost human.

She stood there, rooted to the ground, fear making her skin crawl. If Maggie had been home, Jenny would have run at once to the big house, but her aunt had left hours before. The choice was very simple—either she go back, try to find Massukuntna to come with her, or else go alone.

It came again, full of agony. *Snares*, Jenny thought suddenly, horror washing over her. She began to run toward the direction where the children had gone before they began crying. Here, the foliage was thick and dense; heavy bushes were bowed low with rain and the tall trees hid the clearing. Jenny pushed her way through; a bush scratched her face and she very nearly cried out.

Then, she had reached the clearing, a wide expanse of trampled weeds and half-eaten grass, surrounded on all sides by a fence. It was raining much harder now; the rain pelted her arms, her face, making it almost impossible to see but a few feet ahead. She walked on, then stopped, her skin chilling, as the terrible, keening sound came once again.

There seemed to be shadows, huge, hulking forms huddled in a group, about a hundred yards away. Still squinting through the rain, she saw that they were not shadows but elephants, females, and one of them was half-crouched on her forelegs. Thinking the beast might have been hurt, or was sick, Jenny walked on, but cautiously; Maggie had warned her strongly about getting too close to wild animals, even to take pictures.

But as Jenny got closer, the huge beasts moved away, all but the one who still crouched, looking almost as if it were doing some kind of well-learned circus trick. The cow saw Jenny and raised its trunk; the ear-piercing sound came once again.

Jenny knew she had moved too close, but something, some deep desire to help if she could, had driven her on. And now, now that she was this close, she saw: It was the baby elephant, the one she had called Peanuts, dead, lying on its side, the wide little legs already stiffened in death.

She made some sound, a gasp, a half-sob, and moved even closer. The mother cow made no move, but watched her from its tiny eyes. Jenny, her eyes misting with tears, crouched to look more closely at the dead elephant.

It clearly had been shot. The wound was plainly visible, between the eyes.

Jenny went no closer. She turned and walked back toward the lodge, remembering only after she'd reached the porch that Maggie had warned her never to turn her back on any of the animals. Apparently, the cow had not wanted to leave her dead baby, or else the poor thing had been so filled with grief that even a human presence posed no threat to her just now.

The children were in the kitchen with Manguana. Mugs of hot tea were on the table; little Mozam had stopped crying, but he looked at Jenny with big, sad eyes as she came in.

"Did they tell you, Manguana?"

"They told me, Missy. Better have tea, you are very wet and cold."

"Who did it? Do you know who possibly could have—"

"People from the lodge did it. My people kill and poach, but not with guns. People from the lodge did it, the rich ones who go there and spend money to hunt."

"But—this is a reserve! And that was a *baby* they killed, only a week or so old! How could they—how dare they—"

Manguana shrugged. She did not seem particularly moved; her face was impassive.

"Better a bullet than a snare, Missy. Death comes to all, and to weep for the dead is foolish. Come and have tea."

Jenny took a deep breath. "No," she said, and her voice trembled so that the children stared at her, as if waiting for her to begin crying. "No—I'm not going to—to just sit back and let them get away with this!" She had taken off her raincoat, now, she reached for it and put it on again. "If my aunt gets back before I do, please tell her I've gone to the lodge; tell her I've gone to tell Damien Lear exactly what I think of him!"

Without waiting to hear Manguana's called-out warning, Jenny turned and ran through the house, through the long, chilly hallway, down the steep porch steps, to the parked Land-Rover at the side of the house. Maggie had given her a duplicate set of keys so she could drive into the nearby village anytime she wanted with the children; now, her trembling hand turned the key in the switch and in seconds, she was roaring down the gutted, narrow road leading from the house to the wider but unpaved village road.

Her mind was churning with rage; she drove too fast in the blinding rain, and only the built-in stability of the vehicle kept her on the road as she made a sharp turn. *Calm down*, she told herself, and, taking a deep breath, she slowed down somewhat, reaching to the front panel to turn on the defroster so she could see better. She had no clear idea as to where the lodge was; Maggie had pointed vaguely to the south once, her manner scornful when she spoke of it—or of Damien Lear—and it was in that direction that Jennifer drove now, past the brimming rain forest, past the side road that, she remembered, led directly to the tiny village where Maggie bought fresh produce and flour for Manguana's kitchen.

The road had improved considerably; it had been covered with asphalt and widened. Jenny slowed down and peered through the rain-swept windshield; a sign, neatly painted, announced that Safarilandia Lodge was five miles ahead. She began driving again; signs along the way welcomed the tourist, announced a large sauna bath, three indoor swimming pools, rooms with air-conditioning and a direct communications system to the States and all of Europe. Her rage increased when she read the last sign before the lodge came into view: *Wild animals may be viewed through glass from the convenience of our bar and lounge.*

She pressed down harder on the gas pedal and rounded a final curve. Suddenly, she was in full view of the lodge; it sat in a large grove of trees, surrounded by what appeared to be thousands of blooming orchids. There was a wide, wraparound porch with tastefully placed lounging chairs; the green-and-white-striped awnings of some sort of metal material kept the rain off those people who lounged out there. White-coated servants carried trays back and forth, and a young black girl wearing a long flowered dress pushed a food cart from one lounging guest to another. The entire effect was like something out a dream, a veritable modern palace in the heart of the jungle, hewn wood and polished glass and plush furnishings in the middle of one of the most primitive parts of the world.

Jenny wasted no time. She parked the Land-Rover directly in front of the porch, ignoring the polite sign forbidding parking there, and raced up the porch steps. The girl in the flowered dress paused in serving some sort of iced drink to a balding man smoking a large cigar; she reached out to stop Jenny, but Jenny merely pushed her hand aside and hurried through the ornately carved front door into the vast, carpeted room beyond.

34

This was a sort of lobby, discreetly decorated. A series of couches were placed around various huge, ceiling-high stone fireplaces, and from one of these, a dark-haired man wearing a neat tropical suit advanced toward Jenny. He was perhaps fifty, smiling, but clearly determined not to let her go any further.

"May we help you, Madame?"

"I came—I want to see Damien Lear."

"I'm afraid he isn't in. He's in Nairobi at the moment. Perhaps Madame would care to leave some message?"

She took a small breath. "I'll wait for him, thank you."

"I'm afraid Dr. Lear won't be back for at least several days, Madame."

Jenny looked at him, into his eyes. They were oyster-colored, and something flickered in them; he was lying, she felt sure.

"Tell Dr. Lear," she said quietly, "that if he doesn't see me at once I shall make such a scene that all of his guests will get in their fancy cars and drive straight to the airport!"

"Madame, I'm afraid I must ask you to leave at once."

"I mean it," she said evenly. "I'm here to see Damien Lear and I know he's here somewhere!"

The man reached out and closed one hand over the upper flesh of her arm, not hurting her, but holding onto her very firmly. His face was close to hers, she could see the small veins in his face.

"I'll escort you out the rear door, Madame—if you'll just—come right along with me—"

"I will not! Let go of me—*let go of me!*"

People sitting in the room, some reading, some drinking, smartly dressed and tanned, all of them, stared. Jenny, her left arm in the man's harsh grasp, suddenly drew back her right arm and raised it, preparing to smash her small hand into the man's nose.

35

In that second, a door opened on the far side of the room. A tall man wearing white jeans and an open white shirt stood there; the man who had hold of her suddenly released his grasp. The tall man in the unbuttoned shirt walked swiftly across the room; a smile had come on his handsome, tanned face. When he reached them, he put out his hand and took Jenny's; she looked up at him, into his clear blue eyes, startled.

"So," he said loudly, for everyone to hear, "you've come at last! I'm honored. Won't you come inside for a drink?"

And, his arm around her slender waist, he led her across that wide room, through the open door and into a large, obviously private office.

THREE

For a few seconds, they stood facing each other, Jennifer and the tall, deeply tanned man with the dark hair and the strikingly blue eyes. She was furious, breathing rather hard from her ill-concealed anger and the quick rush this man had given her from the outer room into his office.

For his part, he looked somewhat annoyed, but his hands had left her and his eyes began to look more amused than angry.

"Do you mind telling me what this is all about, Miss?"

Jennifer tried to keep calm, but even her voice was trembling:

"Someone from your hotel—or whatever it is—killed a baby elephant last night, or very early today. Maybe you already know about that—maybe shooting week-old animals is your idea of fair game, good sport, having a fun time! How much money do you get paid to allow people to trespass, how much does it cost those people out there to rent a gun from you, climb a restraining fence and take aim at a poor little—"

"Now wait a damned minute!" He was scowling; his eyes looked bewildered but there was a rising spark of rage in them. "Just calm down a minute and try to make sense! Nobody from my—hotel—as you call it, rents guns, in the first place, and I know better than to set foot on that bleeding-heart game reserve, because if I did, your sweet little aunt would blow my head off as soon as she saw who it was! Furthermore—"

"How dare you talk that way about—" Jenny stared up at him. "How did you know she's my aunt? How—how did you know who I am?"

The ghost of a grin touched his mouth. He went over to a small, portable bar, his back to her, and began mixing drinks. He was a big man, powerfully built, wide-shouldered and slim-hipped, with a broad chest with curly hair on it. With the open shirt, sleeves rolled up, feet bare, he looked more like a man ready to do some kind of bush work in the sweltering sun than the owner of what was reported to be thousands of acres in rich fertile bottom land surrounding his lodge.

"The bush is like a small provincial town," he said, his voice matter-of-fact. "News travels fast." He turned around, a glass in his hand. "It isn't every day a beautiful girl moves into our midst. Of course I heard about you. Besides, you're driving your aunt's souped-up Rover; I saw you when you drove up. Here, have a drink and calm down. I'm really sorry about—"

"Sorry! *Sorry!* Is that all you have to say, that you're sorry one of your spoiled guests—"

"Now hold on a minute," he said, his eyes narrowing a bit. "We don't know it was anybody from here, in the first place. And in the second place, I don't think anybody would be so stupid as to poach with a damned gun, I really don't. The people who come here spend one whole day listening to me harp about fair-game rules in this country, and I can't believe any one of them would be stupid enough to shoot a baby elephant, especially on sacred ground, Miss—"

"Logan," Jenny said evenly, "and I don't like the way you say 'sacred ground,' Dr. Lear. My aunt told me what you think of the work being done on the reserve. I guess you said it yourself, a moment ago, when you called us bleeding hearts." She took a small breath. "Are you saying you know nothing at all about what happened?"

"Absolutely. But I'll have it looked into, I assure you. Would you rather have scotch, Miss Logan?"

"Bleeding hearts don't drink this early in the day, Doctor."

He shrugged, smiling at her over the glass. His eyes, it seemed to Jenny, had warmed; it was as if he were actually enjoying himself. *Cruel*, she thought suddenly, *he has no compassion at all—none*!

"Why don't you go for a swim in one of the pools, and by that time, it'll be late enough for you to join me for dinner and a cocktail. That's the least I can do to welcome a newcomer to this mysterious, dark continent."

"No, thank you. I have your word you'll look into that stupid, pointless slaughter?"

"Absolutely." He put down his glass; he was suddenly not teasing, not treating her as if she were a charming child, a "do-gooder" who had made a silly, pointless scene. "But I think you need to learn a few facts about slaughter—as you call it. It isn't easy, when you first come here, to adjust to certain things. Some people never do, and they don't stay around here very long. The ones that do—some of them—get killed in the bush; they step into a snare or they get their head blown off by some idiot tourist, because they're wandering around where they shouldn't be, or else they drink themselves to death out of a sense of impending boredom or doom."

Jenny smiled coldly. "It looks as if you're well on your way, Doctor."

"Who told you about me, your aunt? I'll bet she painted a nice picture." He picked up the second, half-filled glass and sat in one of the large leather chairs by the wide expanse of window. Outside, lush flowers bloomed in the front garden; five or six men were busily pruning and cutting and mowing. A big fountain sprayed water over the backs of sculpted sea lions and leaping, delicate waterbucks. It was a paradise here, or seemed to be.

"Aunt Maggie doesn't gossip, if that's what you're inferring."

"I know that. Listen—in spite of what she may have said about me, about my ideas, I have the greatest respect for your aunt. As a matter of fact, your Uncle Jack and I used to get together every month or so. I'll bet she didn't tell you that, did she? That in a strange sort of way, he and I were friends."

"Dr. Lear, my aunt and uncle dedicated their lives to caring for animals, keeping them from the very thing some monster did last night to that baby elephant. I simply can't believe that my Uncle Jack would—"

"Lower himself to break bread with me?" He grinned. "As a matter of fact, we used to get a little drunk together and warble old Irish songs."

"Uncle Jack wouldn't—"

"Listen, little girl," he said, his eyes darkening with feeling. "You need a few lessons in survival, and I'm not talking about having enough intelligence to stay out of the bush at night; I'm talking about understanding something about the way people feel around here."

"I don't understand—"

"I know you don't; that's just the point. Here, a poacher isn't always looked upon as if he's some kind of murderous monster; a lot of the time, people just aren't that interested. Some of them are, of course, and I understand

39

they're getting to be more and more that way, but I happen to think it's a damned shame. Most of us aren't involved in any way with the idea of conservation and don't want to be. If somebody tried to blow up your precious parks and game reserves, not many people would give a damn. You're holding your game reserves in trust for a nation that would prefer things the other way, the old way." He put down his glass. "And frankly, I couldn't agree with them more!"

"You mean, I suppose, survival of the fittest."

"Exactly, Miss Logan. The Darwinian theory, if you want to be intellectual about it. There's no aesthetic value here in relation to animals, and you and your aunt or anybody else can't change that. Let's face it—in our country, leisure is an important consideration. Here, food and shelter are primary considerations, and the people, a lot of them, honestly believe they have a natural right to hunt and kill for food and clothing, and for money to take care of their needs. If you and your auntie don't happen to like that—it's just too damned bad!"

Jenny felt her face growing hot. "I don't like it and I won't accept the idea that, like it or not, nothing can be done to change things!"

He came closer to her. "Do you have any idea what would happen if nobody ever killed an animal here? Do you realize that there would ultimately be no grass, no trees, nothing left of this land except starving animals who would eat their own kind to survive? You have to crop excess, Miss Logan, or else even the strongest and the healthiest will perish."

"That baby elephant wasn't strong enough yet to protect itself! It wasn't—it wasn't fair and you can't convince me that it was!" She had not meant to do this, to begin to cry; she hated herself for the tears that had formed inside her, deep inside her, coming hotly into her throat and finally

40

streaming out of her eyes and down her face. "How can you stand there and try to convince me that it was right to kill that elephant?"

"Damn it to hell, girl, I'm not saying that! I'm saying that you can't stick wild animals inside a fence and pretend you're doing them a big favor because there are other facts you have to consider, facts you simply can't change, believe me."

"I'm going to try," Jenny said, wishing she could wipe her eyes, her face, blow her nose and leave with some semblance of dignity. "I'll be waiting to hear from you, Dr. Lear. I assume I have your word as a gentleman that you'll find out who killed our little elephant."

"You do indeed, Miss Logan."

"Good day, then."

She started out, but at the door, his voice stopped her.

"I'll get someone to drive you home."

"No, thank you. I drove myself here and I managed just fine."

"Whatever you like. Ah—Miss Logan?"

"Yes, Doctor?"

He seemed to be looking at her with a new gentleness. "Here," he said, walking toward her. "Blow your nose."

And he handed her a lace-edged handkerchief. He had taken it from a drawer someplace; it obviously belonged to a woman. There was the expensive scent of musk about it.

She drove back slowly, feeling somewhat confused, not sure if anything had been really settled at all. It probably had not, and by the time she drove through the wide gate leading to the reserve, she had come to the conclusion that Damien Lear had very likely been absolutely honest with her; he really didn't have the same feelings about protecting animals that she and Maggie did, and he saw nothing wrong in his viewpoint whatsoever. She must, she reasoned, have sounded like a stupid, naive fool, standing there saying that she meant to change things, when she had only been here such a short time.

Perhaps, she told herself, she ought to apologize to Damien Lear for having been so emotional.

The children went about like small, tearful ghosts, not wanting supper or games or anything else, it seemed. Manguana had bread in the oven and that house was quiet and freshly cleaned. Jenny took her typing to the porch, settling herself there with a glass of lemonade and began her day's work, typing requests for straw, feed, watering bins, and first-aid supplies.

But her mind wandered. She kept seeing Damien Lear, his eyes. She had never seen anyone with eyes that blue; they were clear and candid, changing color from the color of a brilliant sky to a much darker, deeper color. She certainly had not expected him to be so—so—

Attractive.

Suddenly, she stopped typing and sat up a bit straighter in the hard chair. Yes; it was true—she had been attracted to him and part of her confusion and ready tears had simply been a reaction to that! What was she anyway, some foolish, love-starved female who wept with desire at the sight of a man's bare chest, at the look of his face when he smiled? If that were true, then she had better get the next plane back to New York! At least she would have a choice of men there, if that was what she needed so badly!

The sound of a jeep or maybe a truck roaring down the road brought her out of her thoughts. For a wild second, she thought it might well be Damien Lear, come to— what? Get thrown off the place by her aunt? Aunt Maggie just might do that.

But it was Maggie driving the jeep; the back was loaded with boxes of supplies and surprises for the children. Jennifer hurried out to greet her and help her unload.

"Stuff to make ice cream in that box," Maggie said.

"And in that one, some absolutely luscious dress material. Oh, and patterns to make stuffed animals for the kids; I thought you might like that, Jenny. Your mother used to write me about how clever you are at sewing. I'm no good at it at all—all thumbs and—" She looked again at Jenny. "What's wrong?"

"Someone shot Peanuts, Aunt Maggie. The children found him this morning."

"Oh God. Poachers, I expect. I'm sorry, honey, sorrier for the poor beast's mother. She'll make dreadful noises all night and for days to come, I expect. We must get the carcass out of there; we don't want vultures swooping around. Come on; let's have a drink before lunch."

"Aunt Maggie, I'm afraid I've done something you might not like."

"Oh? Now you mustn't let this spoil your time here, Jennifer. I expect someone did it trying to hit one of the big bulls and missed, the bloody fool. They hunt for the ivory, you know."

"Aunt Maggie, I got so—so *upset* when I saw what had happened—"

"Of course you did," Maggie said stoutly, going into the house, "and I don't blame you one bit. I remember when Jack and I first came here, there was a darling little monkey that used to sit on our windowsill. I felt sure he was some sort of good-luck omen, and when I found he'd been killed by poachers, I nearly cried myself sick. Jack kept telling me I'd have to get used to things like that happening, but I never have, quite."

"I thought," Jenny said, her voice low, "I'm afraid I felt certain it was someone from Dr. Lear's place. One of the guests."

Maggie turned at the doorway to look at Jenny. "What do you mean?"

"I was—so certain and so angry and—and upset, that I went over there to tell him. To accuse him, I should say."

43

Maggie was silent until the two of them had begun unloading boxes, putting things on shelves.

"So," Maggie said finally, "you met him. Well, I suppose it had to happen. What did you think of him?"

Jenny hesitated. "I believe he's sincere. I don't agree with him, but I believe he thinks he's perfectly justified in the way he thinks. And it has nothing at all to do with money or greed—"

"I see." Maggie's back was to Jenny as she put away flour and powdered milk for baking. "Did he by any chance call us bleeding hearts?"

"Aunt Maggie—"

"He usually does. Well, to be perfectly honest, I'd hoped I could keep you two from meeting."

"But—why? He's a very intelligent man, and I'd think you'd be pleased to have a doctor fairly close at hand."

"Damien doesn't practice any longer, Jenny. He hasn't for some three and a half years. Besides, I've never liked him because I don't happen to agree with anything he believes in. The very idea of that place he owns, that expensive, moronic palace where people pay a lot of money to sit around, get drunk and go out and kill animals! Oh, I know what he told you, most likely, that hunting with a gun is more fair, more decent than killing with arrows or traps, but all the same—"

"He didn't tell me that, Aunt Maggie. He only wanted to explain some things to me, but I'm afraid I got rather emotional and left."

"I see. Well, it's just as well. My advice is to conquer any feelings you might be having for the man and concentrate instead on your life and your important work here, my dear."

Jenny felt her face flush. "I don't have any—any particular feelings for him. And I'm very happy here."

There was a brief, rather uncomfortable silence. Then Jenny's aunt came over and gently touched her hand.

44

"I'm sorry, dear. I guess I'm getting used to being alone, or at least I'm finding I can bear it, and I forget that young people ought not to live their lives without someone to share it with. I just don't want you to get involved with the wrong man, that's all." Her blue eyes were steady and kind. "I expect you've done that already, haven't you? Isn't that why you came here so suddenly?"

Jenny expected this question; it had only been a matter of when her aunt would get around to asking it.

"Yes," she admitted, "I was—involved with someone. But not to any degree that—what I mean is—I—we—didn't—"

"But you thought about it. Am I right?"

"Yes; I thought about it. A lot."

"Well, what on earth was wrong with him? Why didn't you marry him?"

"He didn't ask me."

"Oh."

Jenny began putting boxes of crackers away. She hoped the conversation had ended; she very nearly changed the subject to ask about whether or not it was time for the children's daily treat of crackers and some of Manguana's honey butter, but Maggie was clever; she'd know there was more to the story.

"Jennifer?"

"Yes, Aunt Maggie?"

Maggie put the last of the candy treats in the cupboard and closed the door. "A girl who looks the way you do—it just doesn't make sense for a man not to want you."

"I told you—he wanted me. He just didn't want to marry me." She took a small breath. "I didn't want to marry him either."

"I see. Then, that means he couldn't marry you, doesn't it?"

"Yes," Jenny said, her voice low. "He—he was married, Aunt Maggie." Sudden tears flooded her eyes. But this time, they were not the same; there was no pain connected with them, only a deep sense of remorse. "I didn't mean to feel about him the way I did; I guess I was horribly lonely without Mother. This was my first job, and in the beginning, he was just very kind to me, that was all. I—I had this room at first, just a room, in one of those dreadfully dreary little hotels where people sit around in the lobby and watch television together at night, and I used to do that, only—only they were old and there I was, just turned twenty, and I didn't have any friends my own age—" She sat down at the table, folding her hands, which had started trembling. "Brendon began taking me places, showing me a different view of New York. I knew it wasn't right—I didn't let myself admit it was wrong, but I certainly knew it couldn't be right, even though he told me his wife didn't mind, that she often went to lunch or dinner with a man friend." She closed her eyes, hating the memories. "He was lying, of course. One day—one day I was shopping on Fifth Avenue; I couldn't afford the outfit, but I'd been given a nice raise, probably as a part of his whole plan about me. Anyway, I was looking at this dress, standing in front of one of those three way mirrors, and I—I glanced up and there he was, Brendon, sitting calmly in a chair with a lady sitting next to him. They were watching their daughter try on coats. She—the daughter—was about my age, very pretty, and his wife kept smiling and leaning close to him to ask him if he liked it. And Brendon just sat there ignoring me, his face kind of pale, but other than that, he didn't let on." She shook her head. "I quit the same day. I just didn't go back to work, and that's when I decided to come here."

"It's over now," her aunt said kindly. "Best to forget it all, Jennifer. Look—let's do something special this evening, shall we? I know you get bloody bored doing nothing but sitting around with an old lady like me—"

"You aren't old! Not at all!"

"Well, it's selfish of me to expect you to be satisfied feeding animals, typing reports, and dozing on the front porch. Tell you what. Put on your best dress and we'll go to dinner!"

"All the way to Nairobi?" Jenny's eyes had widened.

"If you like. We'd have to stay the night, though, and I'm afraid that wouldn't be a good idea, since we've got two bushbabies about to give us more bushbabies. Let's give it some thought, though."

Jenny didn't want to miss helping out when the bushbabies were born; she found them charming creatures, with their huge black eyes and curling tails, they looked rather like honey bears crossed with raccoons. At any rate, to go so far away might mean she'd miss out on helping. She had spent one entire day getting the bedding ready for them, washing down the shelter, while monkeys and other bushbabies and even the shy zebras who usually grazed nearby wandered over to watch her with interest.

The heavy rain kept up all day; children napped on mats on the porch and Massukuntna and Manguana dozed in rocking chairs nearby. At teatime, Maggie fixed a sturdy, fragrant pot of scented tea and carried it in to Jennifer, who was busily typing up a series of complaining letters, composed by her aunt, about yet more snares found at the east edge of the reserve.

"I've come up with a marvelous idea," Maggie said, seating herself comfortably across from her niece. "Why don't we go to Damien Lear's lodge for dinner?"

Jenny stared at her. Her heart had begun a slow, heavy beating.

"But I thought—you said you don't like him!"

"True, dear; I don't, not at all. But you're going to be hearing a lot of different stories about him during the time you're here, and of course, you'll be curious about him, I'm sure. I think it's best we go and let you have a good look at his place, see how fancy it is, how expensive, and then, when all's said and done, remind yourself, Jenny, remind yourself over and over, that the whole place is paid for in the blood of innocent animals!"

"I don't think we should go," Jenny said quietly. "Not after what you've told me about that place."

"My husband thought Damien was sincere in the way he feels about hunting, that he had a kind of—spiritual feeling about it, the way Hemingway used to feel about bullfighting. Maybe he does feel that way, but we're still on opposite sides of the fence with him, Jennifer, and don't you ever forget that."

"I'll try not to, Aunt Maggie." She felt uneasy, as if a part of her were going one way and a part of her the other. The truth was, she was very much attracted to Damien, and this fact surprised her, so soon after her bad time back in New York. But there was something else, she felt certain, some other reason why Maggie hated Damien so. But when she asked, Maggie merely shook her head.

"Because he wasted his life, I suppose. I don't think it's my place to talk much more about it, Jenny, but I do want you to have dinner with me at his place tonight. Jack and I used to go there once in a while; he said it wouldn't be neighborly if we didn't. Besides, he liked Damien, in spite of everything."

"And what *is* 'everything'?"

"You'll hear the gossip, soon enough. I'm trying to think of what to wear," Maggie said, as if it were all definitely decided; they were going. "I haven't worn a dress since Jack's funeral. He always said being married to me was like being married to Huck Finn."

"I've already seen the place, don't forget, Aunt Maggie. There's really no point—"

Maggie smiled. "This time, you won't be going in like some woods animal who is hopping mad. You'll go as a guest, as a well-dressed, lovely young lady. And just keep remembering that if they didn't have those people around there who love to shoot animals, the place couldn't stay open a month!"

It was clear that her aunt was choosing up sides; Jenny would be expected not to like Damien Lear at all, which was going to be a bit hard to do.

She finally stopped her typing. She felt she was beginning to understand both her aunt's side of the problem and at least get a glimpse of how people like Damien felt. Poaching was a terrible thing; they both agreed to that. It was only that Maggie wanted to protect ("over-protect," some called it) the wildlife and men like Damien believed in hunting as a natural means of keeping the species limited enough so that there was no starvation.

But as long as women went on buying fur coats and leather handbags and jewelry made of teeth and tusks and other parts of animals, Jenny knew there would be poaching.

She finally turned her mind to other things; what to wear, to begin with.

She took a rain shower in the stall, where Maggie had left a fresh bar of hard-milled soap scented with the fragrance of wildflowers for her. The water soothed her, made her feel relaxed, and when she went to her room to dress, there was a small glass of sherry on a tray waiting for her.

She had chosen an apple-green dress, a silk print with tiny butterflies on it in darker shades of green and gold. One of Maggie's pretty shawls, a rich cream color, hung on the door. Jenny dressed, then sat down to brush her long auburn hair. In spite of the cooling shower, her face still had that excited, flushed look. She determinedly reached for a box of Maggie's face powder to cover her burning cheeks, then decided against it.

She touched perfume—expensive, seductive—at her throat and wrists. She had bought the fragrance to wear to the theater in New York with Brendon; when she had suddenly decided it was all a hideous mistake, the perfume had remained unopened until now. It was lovely—heady and touched with musk, not unlike the scent of the jungle itself on some warm nights.

"Aunt Maggie!" Jenny exclaimed at the foot of the stairs. "You look just beautiful!"

Maggie was waiting for her; she had turned to smile at Jenny as her niece came down the stairs. Indeed, Maggie did look pretty in the soft lamplight from the hallway; her red hair was pulled back from her face and tied with a pretty silken scarf and she'd touched her cheeks with a bit of rouge.

"I've almost forgotten what it feels like to wear a dress," Maggie said. "Mmmm—you smell delicious, dear. And of course, green is your color." She suddenly looked worried. "You're beautiful, Jennifer. Please take care not to let Damien Lear overwhelm you. Not that he isn't used to having plenty of women, all he wants, I hear. That place of his is a regular mecca for the rich and idle. Come on, we don't want to be on the road in total darkness."

On the trip there, however, it was nearly dark, not because the hour was late, but because the rain and storm clouds threw great shadows across the plains over which they drove. In back of them, the rain forest had looked black and somehow threatening. Sitting beside Maggie in the Land-Rover, Jennifer realized how vastly uncomfortable she felt about this trip. Maggie clearly despised Damien Lear, and he would no doubt be surprised, if not shocked, to see her walk into his lodge!

"Are you sure you don't want to go into the village, Aunt Maggie?"

"Can't hear you. This darned contraption needs a tune up."

"I said—are you—" Jennifer stopped talking; a lioness had suddenly appeared at the side of the road and was watching them lazily. Jenny sat back, giving herself up to the idea of an evening at the lodge. It had certainly been a change from what she'd become accustomed to since she'd come here; Maggie's big house was comfortable but it was impossible to read very well by the feeble, flickering light of the candles and rush lamps, so Jennifer was usually in bed quite early. The long nights were filled with eerie callings and raspings from creatures outside, and until the heavy rains came, she would often settle herself on the porch, where the air was cooler than in the upstairs bedrooms, and where she could enjoy the scented air, heavy with the fragrance of gardenias.

It was a world—a life—apart from the real world, a world where the children and the animals needed caring for, and where she could give of herself without having time to think much about what the future might hold for her in a place like this. But now, suddenly, her aunt was forcing her to look again at the "real" world, a world filled with grown-ups, not innocent animals and children but instead, sophisticated men and women who, much like Brendon Miles, were interested mostly in worldly things— money and sex and power.

She wasn't at all sure she could handle it. Not yet. Not after what had nearly happened to her in New York.

A canopy had been put up in front of the lodge, running the full length of the porch, so that guests could sit out there and enjoy the magnificent view without getting wet. The whole building was second- and third-story level, so that there was a fine view of the lake. In weather such as this it appeared to be gray and foggy, but none the less, the view seen through sparse, pale green grass was magnificent.

A young man wearing a white coat hurried out to park the Land-Rover, and Maggie, giving Jennifer a quick wink, tipped him and walked calmly, and with a grace Jenny hadn't noticed before, up the wide porch steps and through the great, polished ebony doors into the foyer.

At once, they seemed to be surrounded by employees—did they have a reservation, would they like drinks served on the porch, perhaps they would like to be seated in front of the fireplaces since the rain had chilled—

Maggie chose the fireplace; there was a small table between them and a fire burned just brightly enough not to overwhelm them. From her vantage point, Jennifer could see the bar; it was packed tight with well but casually dressed men, and women who looked tanned and, in most cases, very wealthy. Mostly, the women wore low-cut, summery dresses; they sat on the leather bar stools with their tanned legs exposed to the thigh; a few of them wore dresses so sheer one could see their breasts.

Jennifer sipped her brandy, trying to concentrate on what her aunt was saying—something about poaching, and expensive guns that could be bought by the guests right here at the lodge. *So this is his world*, Jenny thought, watching a beautiful woman with very bleached blond hair walk unsteadily toward the closed door of Damien's office. As Jenny watched, the woman tapped at the door, holding a champagne glass in one hand and her shoes in the other. The door opened; Jenny got a glimpse of Damien as he spoke briefly to the woman then started to abruptly close the door. The woman was pouting; she finished her drink and moved toward him, dropping one shoe as she did. She wore a black cocktail dress that showed off her body, showed too much of it; her breasts seemed about to pop out of the tight bodice at the top.

Damien bent over politely to retrieve the fallen shoe; as he did, he glanced quickly around the room. Jenny saw him start in surprise as he saw her aunt sitting there, then he quickly looked at Jennifer.

She sat very still, returning his steady gaze. Even from where she was, the brilliant blueness of his eyes almost dazzled her; she felt captivated in that glance, held as if she were bewitched. Then, the magic moment was over; he handed the shoe back to the blond woman, said something to her in what appeared to be a good-natured way, and quickly shut the door in her face.

"Are you all right, Jenny dear?" It was Maggie, who was busily studying the ornate menu. "You look a bit pale."

"I'm fine," Jenny lied, and she picked up her menu and tried to read it.

It was written mostly in French; many of the guests were wealthy landowners from the Congo, according to Maggie. A thin soup and tiny tidbits of puffy bread had been brought without their asking, but Jenny felt as if she couldn't eat anything; her heart had begun that slow, heavy pounding again, as if she were waiting for something wonderful to begin.

"Don't look now," Maggie said quietly, "but I think we're about to get the V.I.P. treatment."

A tall man wearing a white suit was heading for their table. He carried with him a bucket full of ice with a bottle in it. He made a somewhat formal bow and smiled at them.

"Compliments of Dr. Lear, ladies. He would also like to know if you would care to have dinner in one of the more private rooms. I'm sure you will find the view even more lovely."

"Well," Maggie told him, "since the view from here shows us only the rear-ends of people sitting at the bar, I expect that might be an improvement." She picked up her purse. "Ready, Jennifer dear?"

"Aunt Maggie, I'm quite comfortable here."

"Nonsense. If Dr. Lear wants us to have dinner in one of his special rooms, I don't see why we shouldn't take him up on it. Lead on, my good man."

And so they followed the man in the white suit, who carried their bottle of champagne, up a polished flight of beige-carpeted stairs, into a breezy hallway with oil paintings of scenes of African wildlife on the walls, through a softly lit and beautifully furnished anteroom, into a some-

53

what small but very lovely dining room. There, in front of a glass wall, a table had been set for two. Beside each plate there was an orchid, delicate and creamy-white, huge, exquisitely beautiful.

"Are you sure these are for us?" Maggie, even Maggie, seemed somewhat overwhelmed.

"Dr. Lear suggests the venison for dinner, Madame. He asked me to hasten to add that the meat was not trapped or shot by poachers but sent in from Salaam."

"No meat, thank you," Maggie said. When the man had bowed again and left, she turned to Jennifer. "He's up to something, Jenny!"

"Aunt Maggie, let's just enjoy his generosity and leave as soon as we can." Jennifer stood by the glass wall, looking out. The rain came down like a thin, silver veil, but there was still a good view of the lake beyond. From her vantage point, she caught sight of some large vessel moored at the dock; lights blinked on and off from it. "Do some of these people come here by boat, do you think?"

"That's Damien's yacht out there," Maggie said. "He uses it for gambling, I understand. It isn't something I'd be interested in, even if I could afford it. Are you beginning to understand what I'm trying to tell you, Jennifer?"

Jenny could see people getting on that boat; there was a kind of gangplank on it, with an awning over that, and at the top, someone in a white coat was greeting them. She couldn't hear sounds because of the heavy, insulated glass, but whoever they were, whatever they were doing on the boat, they seemed to be having a marvelous time. As she watched, the lights from the boat shone through like beacons.

Jennifer realized she was very curious about Damien, about why he had chosen to come here to Africa to live. It was, at best, an odd choice, for a man, a doctor, to shut himself off from the world and spend his time doing whatever it was he now occupied himself doing. Certainly, he was living in the very lap of luxury, with his yacht out there, and all the beautifully dressed, mostly good-looking people who were staying at his inn.

And yet, she had sensed something about him, some kind of muted loneliness that had spoken to her heart.

They were brought chilled champagne, waited on as if they were grand royalty; the room was subtly luxurious and the view beyond—the sea and the blinking, colored lights of the pier and the moored ship—beautiful. It was most certainly a night to remember, although Maggie seemed to have her mind elsewhere.

"I wonder if the people at the reserve remembered to feed the macaws and let the goat in the kitchen for his dish of milk before bedtime." Maggie frowned. "He's grown to expect that bowl of milk; I don't want to upset him."

"They'll be fine, I'm sure, Aunt Maggie. We aren't going to be away all that long."

The meal was so delicious and perfect that Maggie and Jennifer both sent compliments to the chef. The fish was juicy and succulent; the yams frosted with a sweet creamy topping, and the salad crisp and fresh, with a brilliant sauce prepared right at their table. Music filtered in from speakers in the ceiling and the room was just cool enough to be pleasant. Outside, gentle rain pattered at the glass wall; Jennifer kept her eyes on the ship's lights beyond.

They were finishing their meal with aromatic coffee when the knock, soft and polite, came at the closed door.

"Please," Jenny said quickly, "let's leave as soon as we can!" With her aunt feeling as she did about Damien, there was no telling what might be said.

"I'm far too old to be told to mind my manners," Maggie told her. She stood up. "Yes; come in."

It was, of course, Damien; Damien looking tall and wide-shouldered and exceedingly handsome in a lightweight suit and shirt and tie. He stood for a moment in the doorway, his blue eyes carefully avoiding contact with Jennifer's.

"I trust you ladies enjoyed your meal? I hope the champagne was cold enough—we sometimes tend to forget that back in the States everything must be served very cold. Here, one finds a certain pleasure in tasting—warmth. Or perhaps it's only that we become accustomed to it."

"It was," Maggie said, her voice cool, "perfect, Mr. Lear. Now, if you'll kindly arrange to have our check sent in—"

"Please," he said quietly, still from the doorway, "allow me this small concession, Mrs. Harmon. May I—"

"Of course," Jennifer said quickly, glancing at her aunt. "Come in. Thank you for—the flowers and this private room and truly the most exquisite meal—"

"My pleasure." He seemed in that moment to fill the room. He walked over to the glass wall, pulled back the transparent draperies with one hand, and pointed to the ship through the fog. "There's a birthday party going on down there; perhaps you ladies would like to try your hand at the gambling tables." He smiled. "I'll furnish you with chips, of course."

"We don't gamble, Mr. Lear," Maggie said coldly. "Oh—I forgot, it's *Doctor*, isn't it? Tell me, when a man is a physician, is it the same as it is with priests? They say an ordained priest is a priest forever—it isn't the same with doctors, or is it?"

Damien Lear was angry; his blue eyes had frosted noticeably, but his voice remained cordial.

"I'm still a doctor, Mrs. Harmon. Feel free to call me in an emergency, in case you can't get Dr. Du Mond in Nairobi."

"We've managed to keep in very good health at the reserve," Maggie said crisply. "So far, nobody has been shot or maimed by any of your stupid poachers."

56

"They aren't my poachers, Mrs. Harmon. And by the way, I found out who killed the baby elephant."

"I hope you kicked them off your property and sent them packing, Doctor."

"They weren't guests here, unfortunately, so there was little I could do. Some tourists, staying at a hotel in Nairobi. They drove onto the reserve—*your* reserve—and took a lot of pictures, I understand, scaring the herd half to death with their noise. When they started to run—the elephants, that is—the little one was behind and when the idiot with the new gun fired, he missed the big fellow he'd meant to hit. It was all very illegal, of course. They've gone now, back home, leaving their mess behind them."

"How can you be sure of all this, Dr. Lear?" Maggie's voice was sharp.

He shrugged. "One of the men who works for me heard about it. Frankly, as long as you people allow strangers to wander in and out of your place with their idiotic cameras, driving noisy, sometimes dangerous vehicles, you can expect things like this to happen. I keep idiots like that off my land."

"And you charge a very high price to the ones you do let on it, don't you?"

Suddenly, he was furious. "I believe in hunting; you know that. But fairly, not with spears, poison spears that cause an animal great agony." He turned to Jennifer. "I'd like to make my thesis clearer, if I may. Why don't you ladies honor me by staying the night here, and when you're rested, let me take you on a brief tour of the bush tomorrow?"

"There's no need of that," Maggie said quickly. "Come on, Jennifer; it's time we were going. Thank you, Dr. Lear, for a most interesting evening."

"Aunt Maggie—couldn't we—"

"It's out of the question." Her aunt looked at her, then seemed to consider something. "Come by in the morning,

Doctor; Jenny probably would do well to see more of the bush. But don't try to convince her that you're right."

His eyes had darkened with pleasure. "Would you like to go, Miss Logan?"

She smiled at him. In that moment, she felt wonderful; a warmth flooded through her and she felt like hugging Maggie for being so gracious about it.

"I'd love to!"

"See you then."

Maggie was putting her shawl around her shoulders when Jennifer asked the question. They were in the Land-Rover; Damien stood on the porch, having escorted them from the private dining room, through the hallways and the big main room and foyers, to the parking lot.

"Why are you suddenly going along with what he wants, Aunt Maggie?"

Maggie put the vehicle in gear and expertly backed out, turning around, and pressed hard on the gas so they shot forward.

"I'm not. I only want you to see his viewpoint so you'll come around to knowing how right I am." She glanced at Jennifer. "But in the meantime, kindly take care not to fall in love with him!"

FOUR

Outside, the morning sounds of the bush had begun. The rain still beat against the long windows, but Jenny had gotten used to that, just as Maggie had said she would. Rain, falling every hour and minute of the day, finally became a fact of life, so that no longer was it a topic of conversation, but rather something that was simply there, like the lovely, morning scent of gardenias that came to her every morning.

I will be with him today, Jenny thought, opening her eyes, *maybe for the whole day!* She felt a warmth go over her; there was a soft ringing sound coming from somewhere in the house, probably one of Manguana's little bells; she had them all over the house. The bedroom was still darkish, and would be until Jenny pulled open the curtains, and even then the brightest it would be all day would be a kind of dim, silver swath of light across the polished floor.

But it was a lovely, lovely day, and she felt good, young and strong and in some mysterious way, whole again. It was almost as if she had been ill, or hurt badly, and for a long while, the pain was very bad, but then it had begun to lessen and she had known she would one day be free of it.

Now, that had happened. She could feel peace again, and although it had not happened yet, she knew she would even be able to feel joy if given the chance.

Suddenly, she sat up straight, her eyes wide now. *Is it because of him, because of Damien? And if it is—why? I hardly know him and if Aunt Maggie is right, he's a totally terrible man! Besides, why doesn't he practice medicine any longer?* She looked toward the gray window. *Probably even medicine didn't bring in enough money for him!*

She got out of bed, quickly brushed her teeth and splashed her face gently from the night's water in the tin basin, then, giving her hair a very quick run-through, she only glanced at her reflection in the mirror before she ran downstairs for breakfast; she looked very much up for the day and her cheeks were much pinker than usual.

But she felt bothered, somehow, as if she needed to know why it was that the world suddenly seemed—different. Oh, it had been good enough the day before, with Aunt Maggie there someplace, wise and good, the memory of Jennifer's mother forever binding them together, because they had both loved her. She, Maggie, seemed more of an older sister than a great-aunt, more like a saddened little girl than a woman who had lived with a man for nearly forty years and who carried the burden of his death with great charm and courage. Days with Maggie around were good days, right sort of days, but today, today was the first time Jenny had felt this way in what—years? Could it really be years since she had been happy, first losing her mother and then moving away and being lonely and then hurt and lonely once again, because of having met Brendon—could it have been so long since she had been serene and looked forward to life? Well, at last she did again—the coffee put in front of her by Manguana (who must have gotten up really early!) had never tasted quite so wonderful, nor had the rain seemed to have quite the same glimmer about it. The scent of flowers coming in the half-opened back door had never seemed this heady; it was as if everything had been brightened, sharpened, since she woke up and she realized that something or someone had sparked life in her again. And if it happened to be the fact that Damien Lear was perhaps the most sensual, attractive man she had ever seen, then so be it.

Manguana was in the kitchen with some of the children; she gave Jennifer a long look that somehow held disapproval in it.

"Good morning," Jenny said cheerfully. "Everyone is well, I hope."

Manguana got right to it. "Your aunt thinks that your head may be turned around like that of the owl, because of Dr. Lear."

"My aunt has a very vivid imagination." So Maggie had been concerned enough to talk about it, and of course, Manguana was very wise. She had probably guessed the truth, that Maggie was hoping she, Jenny, would hate Damien, that she would never stoop to going anywhere with him, never. And that the only possible obstacle to this conclusion happened to be the fact that Jennifer was lonely and worst of all—lately recovering from a near-affair with a most unsuitable suitor.

"Manguana?"

"Yes?" She was spoon-feeding a small boy who sat in her lap.

"If you—if you hadn't met your husband, if you didn't have Massukuntna and you were alone—"

"Not have Massukuntna?" She put down the spoon. "Life would be very sad without him. He is a man who gives great joy to a woman."

"But if you didn't have him," Jennifer persisted gently, "if you had never met him, never heard of him—do you think you could be happy here?"

There was a long, thoughtful pause. "I would," the older woman said gravely, "have been someone else, you see. I am who I am because what we have found together has made me this way. Otherwise, I would have been very foolish. I would be living in a city, with fine furniture and with the wrong man looking at me over breakfast and supper and tea." She smiled a little. "And I might even think myself very fortunate. But from the first, Massukuntna was different."

"Different? How?"

The child squirmed and finally got down. "My village has a custom—when a girl marries, she is given presents by her man. I was—not one of the pretty girls. I was shy and—"

"I can't believe you weren't one of the pretty ones!"

"Not like the others, not like my sisters. So after a while, I got older, and my father worried for fear nobody would ever ask me. He even thought of taking me away, so that my uncles could find me someone suitable. And then, one day came a tall man from Wankie, near the park. His name was Massukuntna and he worked in the park and was, they said, very good with animals."

61

"On the day he came to marry me he brought with him a donkey. And behind it, another. And behind that one, another—and another and another—all the way, halfway through the village! That was the price he paid for me, you see—he gave my father all of those, such a great price, far more than any other girl I'd ever known had gotten for her father. It was as if he believed me to be a—a very great prize."

They were silent. "Yes," Jenny said softly, "he made you feel priceless and beautiful." Was that, perhaps, Damien's great attraction for her? Last night, he had treated her and Maggie to the most elegant meal she'd ever experienced. He had invited her to see him again today. He had made her feel very, very special.

Going out on the porch with her hot bread and sweetened coffee, she found it hard to imagine old Massukuntna, who sat quietly mending his fishing rod, as the sweet and ardent lover he surely must have been. But they loved each other, that was very evident, so Jenny suspected Manguana probably didn't really miss the life she could have had, a different sort of life in the city, after all. Jenny could not, at this point, imagine one without the other; although they seemed seldom to be together during the course of the day, they were together each night, every night, and Jennifer had noticed some mornings how happy Manguana seemed, like a young girl in love.

The porch was clean-smelling, washed over and over by the rain. There were always many birds out there; they came from the bush during the rainy season to roost on and around the sheltering porch, and of course Maggie saw that they got fat from all the seed she was constantly putting out.

The birds screeched when Jenny came out; she had disturbed the sleep of some of the lazier ones. The morning was calm, gray with rain, and very lovely. She had a sudden urge to paint the morning; she could see the touches of sweet lavender drifting around the edges of the dawn. Yes;

she would order some paints and canvas from Nairobi, or perhaps go and get the things herself, and she would paint, the way she used to do before she got involved with Brendon.

"That you down there, Jennifer?" It was Maggie; Jenny had heard the sharp sound of her aunt's opening the window above. "What in God's name are you doing up at this hour?" There was another sound, drawers opening; she was getting dressed. "Nobody, but nobody, gets up this early except Manguana. Are you sick?"

"I'm fine—I'm having coffee." Jenny had to raise her voice against the sound of the rain. "Come on down!"

Moments later, her aunt pushed open the door and plopped into a chair across from Jenny. "He's upset you this soon in the game, has he?"

"I'm far from upset, Aunt Maggie. In fact, I feel wonderful this morning!"

"That's even worse." Maggie put down her coffee cup. "I hope it's clear to you why I'm giving my approval about this little tour you're to take with Damien this morning. You do understand, don't you, Jennifer?"

Jenny felt her face begin to color. She wanted her aunt's approval, and yet, some of the lightheaded, giddy feelings she'd been experiencing ever since she woke up made it impossible for her to be totally serious.

"Of course. You want me to think of him as a sinister person who detests all animals—"

"This is no time for frivolity, Jennifer. I want you to listen very carefully to what he tells you—and then, you can decide for yourself about our work here. You see, Dr. Lear thinks we're no better than some sort of local zoo, where we pamper animals to the point of their being unable to survive in the bush. So you understand how important it is for you to weigh the facts and come to some decision on your own." Her face looked weary this morning, as if she had slept badly. "I wouldn't want you to give a moment of your life to this work if you didn't believe in it, my dear."

Jennifer got up, went over quickly to her aunt, and gave her a quick, warm hug.

"Forgive me—I guess I wasn't thinking very straight this morning. Look—I *know* how important this work is to you, and I know you'd like me to be in accord with your thinking. It was wrong of me to say you want me to dislike Damien Lear for whatever reason. I know you're above that sort of thing."

"For a while, I'm sorry to say I wasn't," Maggie said, her voice soft in the early morning stillness. "You see, Jack always wanted this life, but in the beginning, I didn't, not at all. When we lost your mother, it was more like losing a daughter than a niece; we were nearly shattered. Jack thought it would be a splendid idea for us to come out here and work, so we did. I hated it at once."

Jenny smiled. "I can't imagine your ever hating it, Aunt Maggie."

"I did, though. Then, one morning, when we'd been here about five years, I got up and sat at that dressing table upstairs and I looked at my face and I realized that some kind of change had come over me since we'd come here. I had stopped feeling bitter about life; I felt free and as if I belonged here, and I'd never felt that way about anyplace we'd lived before. Not only that, but I began to feel very lucky, very privileged, to be able to live the kind of life Jack and I lived here. We worked long hours and we were worn out a good deal of the time but we had both gotten a new kind of peace inside." She pressed Jenny's hand. "That's what I want for you, dear. I want you to start meeting people; I'll take you into town so you can start going to some of the parties and lectures."

But Jenny wasn't interested in meeting a lot of new people, making a social life for herself, not just now. For now, just being a part of the reserve seemed to be enough to give her good feelings about herself and about life.

She still wasn't sure just what part, if any, Damien Lear was playing in her life. But she was glad she would be seeing him later on today; that much she knew.

For her bush tour date with Damien, she put on sturdy jeans and a blue shirt-blouse and tied her long hair with a scarf. Her face remained flushed and glowing, even though at the last minute she splashed it with cool rain water from the fresh pitcher Manguana brought to her bedroom.

When Damien drove up in his pickup truck, Jenny was sitting on the wide porch, feeling much better about things. She would listen to what Damien told her on this little sightseeing tour and then later, she would decide for herself what seemed right and best for the animals.

For a second or two, Damien's physical presence blotted out Jennifer's promise to herself about clear-headedness; she could only think that he looked very big and masculine and strong, as he stood waiting for her somewhat uneasily on the porch steps.

He smiled up at her. "I hope your aunt won't think I've kidnapped you if we go into Nairobi for lunch. Maybe you'd better tell her we'll be coming back later than—"

"I'm not a child," Jennifer said somewhat stiffly. "Aunt Maggie won't worry."

"Good. Then we needn't hurry." He turned to look at her, his blue eyes amused. "And you don't have to tell me you aren't a child. I can see you aren't; any man could."

She said nothing, having felt a sudden rush of pleasure at his words. His truck seemed to be filled with papers, invoices of sorts, memos, hunting magazines sent from the States and everywhere. Jenny couldn't help but notice, however, that there was the lingering aroma of expensive-smelling perfume. Either Damien had very recently transported a female guest someplace, or else he had recently had a woman in his truck for other reasons.

"It gets a little bumpy," he told her, his voice loud over the powerful roar of the truck's motor. "Just hang on and don't panic when we come to the river, okay?"

"A river! Won't—won't we sink?" She was clutching the seat with both hands as they went up and down ravines, into ruts and over bumpy flatland.

"Not in the shallow part. I want to take you over to where the snares are."

"I saw them," Jenny said, closing her eyes as they approached the narrow river. "My aunt—"

"I know; she wrote the commissioner in Nairobi and after due red tape, he'll send somebody to come around and sweep them all up and haul them off. But they'll be back within a matter of days, maybe hours."

"But who puts them back up?"

He began to expertly slow the truck down as they approached the river.

"Traders, mostly, a lot of them Americans. Killing animals and selling hides and tusks and teeth is big business here. Maybe you've already realized that."

Jennifer nodded. Even though it was raining, tourists milled around the park, sitting in campers and various motor vehicles, waiting to snap pictures of the first thing that showed itself. One family appeared to be busily (and wetly) removing the sun roof from their van in order to get better shots of animals.

"Against the law to do that," Damien said grimly. "It's a terrible intrusion, all that popping and flashbulb snapping, heads sticking out of the top of a noisy vehicle. It scares hell out of the animals and disturbs the general habitat."

Jenny kept her eyes straight ahead. "And what about poaching—killing with a gun? Surely you agree *that* disturbs the general habitat in a much more deadly way!"

He glanced at her. "Okay, we'll talk about it, as soon as we cross the river."

She did hold on, knuckles white as he inched the truck

across the swirling, muddy water. Damien looked very calm; he seemed to know just how high the water would get.

The truck didn't falter; they smoothly climbed the bank on the opposite side and went on down the narrow, twisting road. Now the trees were denser, even greener.

Damien looked at her, his eyes very blue and serious. "There used to be real hunters here, men who hunted with a kind of—mystic fairness, the way the Indians at home once did. An animal was revered and every bit of its carcass was used for something valuable, and I'm not talking about money. The hunters used to use the hide, the organs, even the eyeballs. But now, there aren't any hunters of that kind left. Massukuntna used to hunt that way, but I understand he doesn't hunt anymore, not since he went to work for your aunt."

Jennifer realized he had touched on something she did not and perhaps could not understand—man's relationship to the animal he hunted. To her, it was inconceivable that it could ever be a fair match. But nonetheless, she knew now that Damien's feelings about animals—and killing them—weren't as harsh and mercenary as her Aunt Maggie seemed to believe they were.

They began to talk, finally, about the animals. Jenny mentioned how dear it was to her to see the little children at the reserve with their beloved pets. And yet, whenever an animal died, it didn't shock them; they cried, but they accepted death.

"It's different now," Damien told her, driving more slowly now. His voice was deeply quiet as he spoke about hunters and poaching. "Everybody—tourists, foreigners, local people—they don't care about the animals. They hunt with snares, and even when they have a gun, nobody is really safe. Sometimes, they use poison arrows, although it's against the law, of course. I'm talking about the kind that killed your uncle."

67

They drove in silence for a little while. Suddenly, Damien stopped the truck and got out. His face looked pale under the deep tan.

"Damien—what—" She realized she had called him by his first name.

"Something caught back there," he told her grimly. "I think it's a deer. Stay here."

But she didn't; she got out and walked quickly over to where he stood, looking down at the poor thing, a young, beige-colored doe, hopelessly caught in the cruel wire snare. Her leg was twisted and bleeding; blood was everywhere. Her eyes looked glazed and agonized.

Jennifer made some sound, covering her mouth with one hand.

"Oh my God—"

"Get back in the truck," he said harshly. "I can't help her; she's nearly gone. But I can stop the suffering. Go on; get back in the truck, damn it!"

She obeyed, shutting her eyes even tighter at the loud blast from his shotgun. Seconds later, he was in the truck beside her, and they drove on.

"They wait days to come and collect their bounty," he said grimly. "It's bad enough when it's an animal, but last summer, a man died in one of the snares. Nobody came to check and see if they'd caught anything, and when they did—"

"Please," Jenny said, her face in her hands. "Please—"

"You'd better get used to things like that," he told her quietly. "Otherwise, you'll hate it. A lot of people hate it, but a lot of people stay because, in some strange way, they love it here. With all its faults, all its problems, this is still one of the most beautiful places in the world." He glanced at her. "Killing is a way of life here, Miss Logan."

"I can't accept that," Jennifer said, her eyes on the road ahead. "It's just too—"

"Cruel?" Suddenly, he pulled the truck to one side of the

road and looked at her. "Life is cruel, or haven't you found that out yet? Survival is what counts."

Jennifer turned to look at him; her eyes were misted with tears, but in that second, it didn't matter. In the rain the trees outside looked ghostly, twisted; the animals had apparently all taken shelter, leaving the bush empty of any living thing—except for the two of them, sitting side by side in that damp-smelling, warmish truck cab.

"If you believe that," she said softly, "if you really believe that life is that precious—why aren't you practicing medicine any longer?"

Until this moment, she had certainly not meant to ask that question. For one thing, it was none of her business, none at all, and if her aunt had wanted to gossip, she would have talked more about it. Now, with a sinking heart, Jenny realized she had touched upon some vital pain within this man; she had encroached upon a very personal part of himself, so deep and painful that his blue eyes darkened like a stormy sky; there was a certain tightening of his jaw and his strong hands seemed to move slightly on the steering wheel.

"I lost a patient," he said quietly. "Ready to go on, now?"

"Yes—I—I'm terribly sorry I asked."

"A lot of people wonder as soon as they find out," he told her, starting the truck once more. "Most of them figure I just fell in love with money and since I can make a lot more of it accommodating the beautiful rich, I switched jobs, you might say."

Jenny took a small breath. "I don't believe that," she said quietly.

He glanced at her in surprise. "Thank you."

They rode now in comfortable silence, up and down the soaked hills, until at last, they came to a clearing. Again Damien stopped the truck and pointed. "There used to be at least three hundred animals killed every day in those damned snares," he told her. "It isn't nearly that bad now, in spite of what we saw back there. Now, they use poison arrows with seeds of the *Strophanthus* plant."

"Is that—what killed my uncle?"

"No, that was *Acokanthera,* made from the wood bark. It's more potent than the other. Jack knew all about the stuff; we used to talk about it sometimes, about how many people got killed by arrows meant for animals."

"I had forgotten you were actually friends with my aunt and uncle."

He smiled. "Not with Maggie, no. But she always knew I'd like to be, and maybe we would have been, in time. But when Jack died, it changed her a lot. I'm still a great admirer of hers." He got out of the truck. "Come on," he told her, reaching for her. "I want to show you something."

"But it's pouring!"

"It isn't far. I want to show you the rain forest. It's something you'll never forget."

It was true; she would never forget it. Suddenly, with her hand in his, she was led into a giant, emerald room, a room made by the heavy overhead branches, the green, green trees. Inside there was no rain, only the smell of the good brown earth and of the rain itself, washed clean and heavy with the scent of jungle flowers. It was a world in itself, one of those unexpectedly heart-stopping, beautiful moments in time.

Later, Jennifer was to ask herself if it was because of the beauty of the place, the exquisite serenity of the rain forest, or if it was merely because Damien shared it with her that made it so precious, so special to her.

"I've never seen anything like it," she said, standing in the middle of that greenness. "You were right."

He stood watching her; they were perhaps ten feet away from each other but there had sprung between them a kind of swift, electric closeness. She was very much aware of his steady gaze and surprisingly, she was bold enough to meet his eyes without trembling.

"You," he said quietly, "are like nothing I've ever seen. You can't imagine how—how magnificent you look at this moment."

Jenny looked quickly away. She had never thought of herself as beautiful, except for the inherited red hair; that was the pride of all the women in her family. Aunt Maggie had once said that there had only been two brunette girls born into the family in the last century, and, she had added darkly, nothing any good ever came of either of them.

But she was not, and could not be, magnificent to look at, not by a long shot, she with her share of freckles, even on her arms, and her mouth a bit too wide, just like her mother's, only on her mother it had somehow seemed sensual and lovely.

"I must bring the children here some day for a picnic."

"You," he said, coming toward her, "are a picnic—a feast—"

And he was nearly, very nearly, kissing her. There was, coming from the moist air around then, a sweet, heavy scent, mingled juniberries and mint and gardenia, and she felt suddenly dizzy with the sweetness of it, that and his arms around her.

But she suddenly, as if a picture had been flashed on a screen, saw Brendon that day in his office when he had told her how much he lusted for her, how he had wanted her from the first day she worked for him. . . .

"I think we'd better go," she said now, turning, half-twisting away from him. He suddenly looked bereft, then; he was changed, and a curtain had come down over his eyes.

"Let me know when you want to bring the children, Miss Logan. I'll send one of my guides along to look after everyone."

She felt uncomfortable for the rest of the afternoon with

71

him. He drove her into Nairobi and they had lunch on the top floor of a white, very modern American hotel. The appetizers they ordered were deplorable and she didn't really want the expensive wine he ordered.

"Listen," he said finally, reaching over, putting his tanned hand over hers. "I'm sorry about what—I mean, I had no right to talk the way I did—say those things. I know I embarrassed you and I'm sorry." His blue eyes looked into hers; he was smiling gently at her. "Okay?"

Suddenly, she looked at her plate. "What makes you think I was embarrassed? Maybe I—liked it." She looked steadily at him. "A lot."

A slow flush was rising on his face. "Then why—I mean, if you wanted me to kiss you, why the devil didn't it happen?" He touched her cheek gently with one finger. "I know I wanted it to happen, but on the other hand," he said lightly, "I don't want your aunt coming around my place with a large pistol, shouting that I've been fooling around with her favorite niece. Let's try for a steak here; I understand they're terrible but I want to see you eat a nice hearty meal."

"I really don't like to eat much meat," she said, feeling that she was suddenly being treated rather like a child that he found charming. "I'll just have the vegetables, please."

"That calls for a drink," Damien said teasingly. "I should have known all bleeding hearts are vegetarians!"

It was dark when she got back to her aunt's; Damien had bid her goodnight quickly and she'd gotten out of his truck, hurrying through the dark rain.

"There you are," her aunt said from the dim living room. There was a burned-down candle in a dish beside her. "Well, I'd given you up. I must admit I had fantasies about your spending the night with him in Nairobi."

"Fantasies, Aunt Maggie?"

"I assure you, I didn't get past the part where he asked you to dance. I understand from some of the people here that in the beginning, Dr. Lear dances with a girl. Holds her close and puts his mouth close enough to her ear so that she can feel him breathing. It's evidently very successful because he's had scores of women, my dear, or have you already figured that out for yourself?"

"I'm going to bed, if you don't mind," Jennifer said, realizing she was unwilling to talk about Damien. "I'm sorry I missed dinner—we had a late lunch. Aunt Maggie—there's something I need to talk to you about, but it can wait until tomorrow. Goodnight." She bent and gently kissed her aunt's forehead. "Sleep well."

"Jennifer!" Maggie had followed her into the hallway. "Now you turn right around and look at me, young lady!"

Jenny turned. "Aunt Maggie, I really don't care to—"

"Didn't he tell you his big-shot ideas about the bushland? Didn't he talk about survival of the fittest, which means he thinks we're all a bunch of dodder-headed busybodies who capture animals and take care of them, whether they want to be cared for or not?" Maggie was clearly angry; her voice was heavier than usual, thickened with wrath. "That's what your Dr. Lear thinks about us, Jenny. Don't you see?" she demanded, and Jenny realized her aunt's voice was wavering. "If Damien Lear is right—if my husband and I worked this hard, this long, just to be some kind of zookeepers—then Jack's whole life was a failure—and mine is too!"

"Damien and I didn't talk much about that," Jenny said. "Please—don't put me in this position, Aunt Maggie. Besides, I don't think it's all that important that everyone agree with everyone else. Life is more interesting when people don't, sometimes."

"It isn't—just that," Maggie said suddenly. She walked up to Jenny and put her arm around her niece's waist as they walked towards the stairs. "It has to do with my husband, you see. Anything that might have saved him makes me start a whole, wild train of thinking. And it's far too

73

late tonight for me to get started on my what-ifs. What if I had made him promise me never to try to come home if he couldn't get here before dark? There'd been a run of poaching about then, natives using the spears dipped in poison—he knew it wouldn't be safe, but he wanted to get back to me." She smiled a little. "He didn't want to break our record."

Maggie was switching on rush lamps, turning them up a bit, so that suddenly, her face was outlined in the soft light. She looked a bit, Jenny thought, like a lonely child, standing there without him, without her husband. They had been together so completely, for as long as Jenny could remember, that it still seemed odd, seeing one of them alone.

"Record? Aunt Maggie—you're stepping on your gown."

"What? Oh," Maggie said. "Yes. This was one of Jack's favorites. Our record had nothing to do with sex, not really, although sometimes we used to make love with a kind of glee, because we'd been able to keep our promise to each other." She took a little, sharp breath. "We made a promise when we first got married that we'd never sleep apart if we could help it. He was trying to keep his promise."

They were very close in that moment. The sense of loss, of grief, was so profound to Jenny that long after she'd crawled into bed and closed her eyes, something was nagging away at her, bothering her. She finally sat up in bed; the thought was coiled inside her mind. She felt she had to find it, grasp it and look at it, because if she didn't, she'd have missed something very important.

She needed to feel as blessed as the women who had fallen deeply in love with one man and stayed that way, through it all, for all of their lives. It was a sort of special blessing, some magic given to some women, to love only once and then forever. Not all women could know it; she had known many women who had been in love various times. Her own mother had had lots of lovers, quite a potpourri, but she hadn't, as far as Jenny could tell, actually been in love with any of them. A lot of people apparently never fell in love at all, not even once.

Am I afraid that will happen to me?

She pressed her face on the pillow to shut out the look of the slanted rain outside. *It might only be that I've decided it's time to fall in love, after a very bad experience with Brendon, and I might just be looking for someone to—*

The thought trailed off in sleep. She dreamed, of course. She was in a great, vast sea, very green, a deep and beautiful green, and she was being sweetly and soundly kissed by Dr. Damien Lear.

FIVE

Things at the reserve were cracking, as Maggie would say, as soon as it was dawn, the following day. By the time Jennifer came downstairs, Maggie had gone with Massukuntna to help with the birth of lion cubs and the kitchen was cluttered and steamy; it was canning time and Manguana silently and with great concentration boiled dark, sweet berries to make jam. Several children, giggling, hid under the big preparing table, waiting for the first taste.

It didn't seem to be the day to discuss her plan with Maggie, even though it kept rolling around in her mind. She longed to talk to someone about it and since Maggie might be gone all day and Manguana was going to be in the kitchen all day, there was no one.

Except for Damien, of course. All morning, typing, pressing the official stamp onto the neat letters, Jenny waited for some message from him. She even thought Damien himself might suddenly drive up in front of the house,

75

big and wide-shouldered, telling her to get in his truck, telling her that he wanted to talk to her about something, or that he wanted to show her another secret place in the rain forest, the way he'd done yesterday.

But there was no word, none at all. She could not get what had happened—nor nearly happened—off her mind, however; she felt foolish for having made a mild fuss about a near-kiss, but still, if she and Damien had kissed, would it have meant anything at all, or would it only have been some unexpectedly dear pleasure, to be taken and then never repeated?

At noon, over a steaming bowl Manguana brought to her (soup, clear, deliciously flavored with herbs and root vegetables grown in the kitchen garden), Jennifer began to wonder if perhaps the tour with Damien had not been a mistake. She was perhaps too attracted to him, and at this point, she wasn't really sure if she belonged here or not. Africa had been a shot-in-the-dark, a place to run to, but now that she no longer thought of Brendon, except with a sense of shame and regret, it seemed to her that her life needed more meaning. She felt she had wasted enough of the precious time of her life, being a part of Brendon's foolish world.

She wanted no more of that.

Jennifer had just finished lunch when Manguana suddenly came in from the kitchen.

"Dr. Lear is here; I told him to wait in your aunt's study."

"Dr. Lear is—here? Thank you, Manguana." Suddenly, she felt a deep sense of joy at the prospect of seeing him once again.

There was no time to primp, to go off to her bedroom and comb her hair or perhaps put on a trace of lipstick. Besides, she had promised herself that she would be very sober and mature about Damien, since her emotions had run away to some selfish never-never land as far as her

76

ex-boss was concerned. Actually, she knew very little about Dr. Damien Lear, since Aunt Maggie had told her practically nothing and didn't seem at all inclined to.

"Well," Jennifer said cheerfully, facing him in that book-filled room, "to what do we owe this honor, Dr. Lear?"

She nearly always forgot how tall he was, how he seemed to fill a room with his physical presence. Today, he wore high hunting boots, black, with the cuffs of his white pants tucked in. The blue denim shirt was casual, with sleeves rolled up over strong, muscled arms.

"Things would be much simpler if your aunt would have a phone installed," he told her, smiling. "That way, I could have called to invite you to lunch."

"I just had lunch, thanks."

"Dinner then, in Nairobi. And this time, I promise you the food will be great. I'm afraid," he said quietly, "yesterday almost turned into a disaster. I acted a little like an overly eager teenager who hadn't seen a girl for ten years."

"I'm sure," Jenny said, beginning to smile, "that nothing could be further from the truth."

"Does that nice display of dimples mean you'll have dinner with me?"

"My Aunt Maggie isn't here and I—there's a lot of work piled up." He waited silently, and suddenly, she burst out: "I have something—a sort of idea—and maybe, instead of talking to my aunt, I ought to be talking to you about it!"

"Sure, I love to listen to people with big plans. Ready to go?"

"Dr. Lear—this is serious! It's about getting the children together—"

"And having a picnic in the rain forest? Great, but not today. Today I want to introduce you to some very nice people, friends of mine. In case," he said, leading her gently but firmly out of the room, toward his waiting truck parked in front, "you're wondering why I haven't chosen

77

my lodge as our place to have dinner, it's because there are so many stupid, boring people wandering around there."

"Listen," she said suddenly. "I—I'm not dressed—if we're going to dinner, I'd like to change. And I'll have to tell Manguana, so she can tell my aunt."

"I guess that means you want me to come back later." His gaze was warm. "Frankly, a girl like you doesn't wander into the jungle every other day. There must be at least fifteen guys at my lodge, guests from various places all over the world, who would love to squire you around." He shrugged his wide shoulders. "Don't forget, mine is the first bid."

And so she had plenty of time in which to shower, standing in the little stall under the warm rain, using the lovely, fragrant soap Maggie always kept on hand, then sudsing her long hair so that it would be fragrant too.

Shortly before she went back downstairs, she heard Maggie come in. First, there was the roar of her aunt's ancient Rover, then the excited voices of the children in the kitchen; apparently, there were presents and surprises for them, as usual.

"Jennifer? I've got you a raincoat; come down and see!"

"I'll be right down, Aunt Maggie." Why did she feel guilty, reluctant to go downstairs?

Her aunt was in the savory-smelling kitchen, with six or seven children tugging at her.

"This doll is for you, Tania, and if you pull off this one's arms, I won't bring you new clothes for her when I go next time. And we've got—let's see—building blocks and—oh," Maggie said, "there you are, Jennifer. Why, you look just beautiful, dear; what a pretty dress. Rather fancy to wear to type up reports, isn't it?"

The dress was sunny yellow, silk and clinging, draping softly over her hips and breasts. She had bought it to wear with Brendon Miles, but thank God, she never did. It was expensive and looked it.

"If it's all right with you, I thought I'd go out."

"Out ? In that? In this rain?"

"Aunt Maggie, could I speak with you a moment?" Jenny's face felt warm; she actually dreaded what she must say. *Dreaded*? Why? and why should she feel so terribly disloyal?

"Of course, dear. Go in the study and I'll show you the raincoat I brought you." Maggie smiled, but her eyes were wary. "I want to finish giving the children their surprises."

When her aunt came into the study where Jennifer waited, Jenny had made up her mind to come straight out with it.

"I'm having dinner with Damien," she said quietly. "I'm sorry if that displeases you."

"I see." Maggie laid a square box on the table and began unwrapping it. "This might seem rather big, but out here, the idea is to cover oneself completely from the rain, you see. They're imported from London, very sturdy—"

"Aunt Maggie, are you angry with me?"

The blue eyes met hers steadily. "I did feel anger, but only for a moment. You see, all my anger is bound up in Jack's memory. Now that Jack is gone—it's terribly important to me to know that the work here is vital. Doctor Lear doesn't think it is. I explained that to you before, Jennifer."

"Aunt Maggie, I don't see that a difference of opinion—"

"Have you ever loved a man, Jennifer? Really loved a man, the kind of love that goes beyond the grave?"

"No. I don't—know anything about love, not really. I've only played at it."

"Then," Maggie said quietly, "you don't have any idea what I'm talking about."

Jenny took a small breath. "I don't want to hurt you. I couldn't do that. If you really don't want me to go—"

"You must make your own mind up about Damien Lear, Jenny. Let's not talk about it anymore, shall we? Here—come and try on your new raincoat."

79

Jenny lifted it from the box. "It's lovely—thank you." Suddenly, she was hugging Maggie. "I promise you, I'll ask questions today. I'll try to understand what his real feelings are about your work here. I'm sure he respects you and I'm sure he was very sorry about Uncle Jack's death. But if he's the way you say he is—cruel to animals, uncaring—"

"I didn't say that, Jenny. I said his ideas about reserves mean that animals must fend for themselves, and sometimes, that means an early death."

"Aunt Maggie—that baby elephant died an early death, and it happened right here on the reserve!"

"Of course. We can't keep the poachers away entirely, but at least we don't have animals starving to death! Out there, the people take the land and plow it and plant it for food, driving the animals out. Or else they graze cattle until the land is overgrazed and destroyed. Or they make a living by putting up snares, so they can sell hides. The farmers say they can't very well have lions roaming around on their farmlands and they can't grow a patch of corn and allow elephants to wander through it, helping themselves, so what they do is build fences—or else they kill whatever sets foot on their land."

"And Damien agrees with all of that?"

"No. He thinks he has another answer, but as I said—it's up to you to decide about him. Well, dear, I'm finished and I smell Manguana's soup simmering. The coat fits you very well. See you later." She turned at the door. "Thank you, Jennifer, for not asking all those questions about him that I'm sure you're dying to ask."

Damien came promptly at five, standing at the foot of the stairs in the hallway, his eyes admiring Jenny as she came down the stairs.

"I asked myself why I was putting on a shirt and tie," he told her, "when my friends in Nairobi will probably be wearing the usual blue jeans and bare feet. Now I'm glad I did."

He took both her hands in his. "That's a fantastically beautiful dress. Or maybe it's just you in it that makes it look so great."

"Did you say we're going to have dinner with some friends of yours?"

He was helping her on with the new coat. "You'll like them. Well, either you'll like them or you'll think they're a little crazy. He's a doctor; she's a nurse. They run a clinic just south of the city. Crazy place—they've got nearly as many animals running around as your aunt has."

The truck was cool; he had left the windows down and he had parked so that the rain and wetness wouldn't blow in. Settled in the seat beside him, Jennifer watched as animals on the reserve scurried to safety as the truck roared by. Several lazy-looking lions perched in trees, watching them as they drove by.

"Fat cats," Damien said suddenly, breaking the silence between them. "Did you ever stop to think that they couldn't survive without people? They were here a long time before we were, you know. Now, they just lie around on tree branches and look stupid."

So that was the way it was going to be! He was going to jump right into an argument and get it going. *Well, fine,* Jennifer thought, *let him! I'm not going back to Aunt Maggie's until I make my mind up about this man—one way or the other!*

"I think," she said quietly, "they look beautiful."

"Well, take a good look," he told her, "because before very long, you won't be seeing them anymore. Even people like your aunt know that they're on their way out. Right now, the signs are all there, but frankly, a lot of bleeding hearts don't want to talk about it. In another fifteen years, Kenya will have about twenty-five million people. They have to be fed, so the animals get pushed off grazing land, out of the bush, even out of game reserves, so food can be grown. It's a losing game." He turned the truck swiftly to

81

the left. Now they were approaching the smooth road leading to the city.

"Dr. Lear—"

"Damien." He glanced at her. "After all, I nearly kissed you yesterday in the rain forest. That makes us buddies, or something, after such a close encounter."

"You said yesterday that as long as people buy fur coats and handbags made out of hide, the poaching would go on. In other words, there's a solution to the problem of poaching."

"Grow up, little girl." His voice was grim. "I could count the number of women I've known on one hand who wouldn't accept a fur coat. Make that one finger." He shook his dark head. "And that lady was my mother. All the others would wear that bushy-tailed impala over there just as soon as somebody could get him shot or hung up in a mesh trap, or maybe caught between the eyes with a poison spear. Skin him, put in a cloth lining and a label and she'll pay a lot of money for him."

It was true; all one had to do was walk down a street in New York at noontime in the winter, past the fancy stores or the chic disco places, and there would be scores of women wrapped up in mink, sable, and other animal furs.

"You think it's hopeless then." She looked at him; his profile, she couldn't help but notice, was lovely, like a piece of sculpture—the strong jaw, the indent that became a smile crease, the good, straight nose, the thick, sooty lashes. "I don't," she told him. "And that's what I wanted to talk to you about. Please, Damien, before you put me down as another bleeding heart."

He looked quickly down at her; his eyes were warm and smiling. "Say that again, please."

"I said before you write me off as what you love to call a bleeding heart—"

"No; not that. My name. It sounds different when you say it."

"Please don't tease me. I'm very serious. I just sort of got this idea yesterday and it's stuck with me. I'm going to talk about it to my aunt, but first—"

"I am serious," he told her, turning his attention to the road once more. "I like it when you say my name."

"Damien—" Jenny folded her hands in her lap; they had begun to tremble slightly. "Haven't you ever considered approaching the problem of poaching from the other side? What I mean is, to educate the children not to—"

"Look!" He didn't seem to be paying much attention to what she had said or was about to say; in fact, he seemed to be treating her rather as if she were a sweet, charming and desirable female, but nobody to be taken all that seriously.

A pack of impalas had reacted to the sound of the truck with their usual quick, soaring jumps. These were beautiful, sleek and black-faced, bounding over the flatland as if they were on strings. To the north of them, Mount Kenya showed itself like a hulking shadow through the rain.

"They're lovely," Jenny said appreciatively. "Damien, will you please listen to me?"

"Of course. You have a beautiful mouth; I like to watch it move over a word. But right now, I'd better concentrate on not running over any of our furry friends."

So Jennifer put the words away, for then, promising herself that at the first opportunity she would talk to him about her idea. At first, the thought of embarking on a plan to help solve the poaching problem seemed a little wild since she was so new here. But it kept bothering her, and there were the children, the children who would grow up to be poachers like their fathers and grandfathers; there would be no end to the grisly, hideous slaying of innocent animals. Unless . . .

The city was in sight at last, low-lying, rather grim-looking in the rain, but very busy. Almost until they entered the city, they had seen wild animals—a small band of elegant zebras had run along side of them for nearly a mile, manes flowing backward in the wind.

Now, Damien turned to look at Jenny. "I'm sorry if I sounded rude back there. But I didn't want you to miss seeing any of the animals. Like I said, if you decide to come back thirty years from now, most of them will probably be gone."

He had parked the car in front of a small café, a crowded, noisy place with an awning stretching out to the front. Tables were set up near the street; nobody had bothered to take them inside when the rains began. Now, he led her inside; holding onto her hand, he went in first, shouldering his way through the noisy crowd. Many of them were office workers from the downtown section, petty officials who had come in to have tea before going home from work. It was a dreary place, with rough wooden tables and limp-looking curtains hanging from the windows.

"Don't be discouraged," Damien told her. "This is the best place in town to get an American beer, black market, of course. Save your appetite for food, though—my friend's wife is a gourmet cook."

"An honor, Dr. Lear," the waiter said, bowing slightly. "You have been too long away from us."

"Busy trying to educate tourists on the fine art of handling a hunting rifle, Saiwan. This is an American friend of mine, Miss Jennifer Logan. This is Saiwan Kairobe, the proud owner of this establishment."

The man grinned and bowed again. "Two cold beers," Damien said, "frosted glasses."

"Damien, I really don't want anything to drink. Just tea."

"Tea for the lady, please." He leaned closer to her. "If the tea makes you dizzy, forget it. Sometimes they spice it with weird jungle herbs."

"Will you kindly listen to what I have to say now?"

"Of course. You're going to save the animals from poaching with a brand-new idea."

Her face flamed. "I know it sounds foolish, as if I'm some—some—"

"Intruder?"

"Yes, that. And worse, an idiot. My aunt, for instance, would probably think, without telling me, of course, that I was a silly, very vain girl to get the idea that I could come here straight from New York, never having been any closer to wild animals than a trip to the zoo, and start spouting ideas about teaching people."

He looked at her, some kind of emerging interest coming into his eyes.

"Teaching people? Are you talking about educating the kids?"

"Exactly." She leaned closer to him, so he could hear her above the general noise of the place. "I heard some of the children talking this morning about animals they'd seen last week, and all the time they talked, Manguana had to tell them they were calling some animal by the wrong name!" It was true; even her aunt had gently reminded one little boy that it could not possibly have seen a cow running in the kitchen garden, since all the wedding cows were always tied up at the house of Manguana and her husband Massukuntna. It must, her aunt had told them, have been a wildebeest. "Damien," she said earnestly, "those children have lived here all their lives—and they can't tell a zebra from a cow or a cow from a wildebeest!"

"I often wonder about that when the meat comes in to stock my larders at the lodge. I'm not sure some of my hunters can tell one from the other. It makes the meals interesting, though—the guests never know whether or not they're eating monkey."

She stared hard at him, then finally she sat back in her seat. Her manner was cool and reserved.

85

"You aren't listening, are you? You can't possibly imagine that there just might be some value in what I'm talking about!"

"Sorry." He was still grinning, still teasing. "Look, nobody gives a damn what they shoot, just so it's edible. It comes down to that. Anything else is pure—"

"Fantasy? Is that what you're thinking?"

"Look," he told her, "if you're going to get mad at me, okay, but—"

"You actually think that it's all well and good for the children not to really care about the animals! Because you don't care, you can't understand why other people do, why children can grow up and change things—"

"I do care, dammit! But I happen to believe the answer lies in a totally different direction from fencing wild animals in, that's all!" His eyes were growing dark. "Tell me, Miss Logan, have you always had some cause to get excited about? I'll bet you carried placards and went to marches back home, right?"

Anger, slow, chilling, began to go through her. "You really do think my aunt and I and everybody else at the reserve are nothing but a bunch of crazies, don't you, Doctor?"

Suddenly, they were furious with one another.

"Frankly," he said, "yes, I do. But that doesn't mean I don't like your aunt and that I didn't respect and admire your uncle a great deal. It simply means that I happen to believe their energies have been gravely misdirected."

She looked quickly down at her cup. The waiter had come over with a large, copper kettle filled with tea; it smelled deliciously fragrant, scenting the moist, warm air around them with the aroma of spices and rose petals.

"Do you have any children staying at your lodge, Doctor?"

"No. I always try to avoid having them around the place."

"I see." She heard her own voice, quietly, relentlessly going on with it. "Are you against children, then?"

"Of course I'm not against children. What the hell is that supposed to mean?"

"It means that you won't show any interest whatsoever in what I have to say, even though you have the power to make my plan possible!"

"If you're asking me to help build a school, the answer is a flat-out no, Miss Logan. I happen to feel that children are not safe here and shouldn't be encouraged to stay. If at all possible, they should be taken out, transported, taken to some place where they aren't likely to die because they stumbled into a poacher's trap, or perhaps get their eyes put out from a poison arrow meant for a gazelle!"

She was silent again, feeling the quick, heated anger flow out of her, feeling a certain relief that it was gone, almost as if she had actually hated having to hate him. It would be so easy to feel something else for this man, something wonderful and exciting.

"Your face is red, Miss Logan. Did I say something to offend you?"

"No," she said softly. "I'm just glad that—I understand where you are. I don't fully, but at least I've got a start." She smiled at him, a beginning smile that began to clear the air about them at once. "You don't think it's safe for children to grow up here?"

"My dear girl, I don't think it's safe for children to grow up anywhere on the face of this earth!" He raised his glass to her. "Here's to a peace treaty until at least dinner tonight? Good." His eyes met hers and suddenly, things were right once more. The argument, the anger, had come about quite unexpectedly; one minute he had been teasing her, and the next moment, she had touched on something vital in him and he'd become coldly furious. Not because he didn't care, she suspected, but because he did care, very much indeed.

She finished her tea, then went into the powder room to freshen up before going on to Damien's friends' place. There was nobody there; the rooms smelled clean and powdery. Jennifer bathed her warm face, then stared at her reflection for a few seconds. Had she ever, in the past, when she was living and working in New York, felt this way about a man? The answer to that was yes; she had thought she was in love with Brendon, all of which pointed to the fact that she was unstable, likely to fall in love far too easily, still upset over her mother's death, still searching for a life of her own, something of importance.

So if this man attracted her, she must remember he attracted many women, dated many women from all over the world, rich, spoiled, beautiful women who came from places like Monte Carlo and Paris and Berlin.

"I think we'd better be going," Damien told her when she got back to the table. "Heller gets very annoyed when people are late to dinner. You'll like her—she's an animal nut too."

Dr. Paul and Heller Du Mond lived in a rather large, airy upstairs flat over a bakery. There was a white-washed balcony with a half-dozen hanging plants, suspended from a wooden rafter roof. The city surged about the building, but once Damien and Jennifer stepped inside the downstairs door leading up a flight of rather dim-looking stairs, the world and sounds were shut off. Jenny stood beside Damien in the small, darkish entryway, her shoulder touching his arm.

He had been peering at mailboxes. "Here it is," he said, turning to look down at her. Suddenly, he very slowly put both arms around her and gently drew her, quite willingly, closer to himself, in the warm circle of his arms.

Neither said a word. Jenny closed her eyes and rested her face against him, against his chest; she could hear his heart beginning to beat very hard.

His hand gently stroked her hair. "Once I found a little

88

wildebeest, caught in a trap just east of the rain forest," he said quietly. "Scared to death—wouldn't let you get near her for a while. But she and I got to be friends because whenever we'd see each other around the lodge, I'd hold her for a while." He smiled down into Jennifer's warm face. "Look at me, Jenny. Do you know what finally happened?"

"No."

"That little devil got so she thought she owned the whole place! She'd bite people if they didn't throw her enough peanuts from the bar. Come right up and snarl at them. Scared a lot of 'em off the premises."

Very gently, she withdrew herself from his arms. "Is that how you feel about women in general?"

"I guess you could say that. Ready to go up?"

The apartment door was not solid wood but instead, a sort of swinging door made of a light material that lead directly into a large, breezy room, a patients' waiting room. Beyond that, Jenny could see a room with a table and medical equipment, and to the right of that, a bathroom with a gleaming white tub. There were hanging plants everywhere, charming wallpaper, and the aroma of a fragrant, simmering stew.

"There you are," a woman's voice said, and Jenny turned to look at her hostess. The woman was perhaps thirty, black and good-looking in a wholesome kind of way. Heller Du Mond wore a large-flowered smock and her hair was tied back in a ribbon, yet one felt instinctively that she was a nurse. "I was afraid Damien had spirited you off to see something he particularly likes. One day he took a pregnant patient he was supposedly bringing to see my husband for a joy ride and she delivered her baby as Damien was pointing out the sights of Lake Naivasha."

"She wanted to get up and walk on home with her baby," Damien said with a slight smile. "Very strong-minded women around here." He glanced at Jenny. "If you should marry here and have children, be prepared to be back at work within twenty-four hours. Otherwise, we'll all think you're a slacker."

A man about Damien's age, probably in his early thirties, had emerged from one of the inner rooms. He was stocky, powerfully built, with a smooth black face and freshly clipped beard. He seemed delighted to see Damien; they shook hands and clapped each other on the shoulder like raucous schoolboys. This was Dr. Paul Du Mond and because he and his wife ran a "twenty-five-hour-a-day" clinic, Jenny soon found herself alone once again with Damien, on a sort of long, comfortable back porch with a view of snow-capped mountains beyond.

"Well, what do you think of their clinic?" Damien sat across from her, holding a glass of wine that Heller had served to them. Night city sounds floated to them; a car horn blared, then abruptly stopped. From inside one of the rooms of the clinic, a baby began crying steadily.

"I guess I imagined a sterile, scary hospital. This place is charming."

"It isn't what we—what they had planned to have, of course." He looked beyond her, out at the lights of the city. "To tell you the truth, after your Uncle Jack died, I found myself wondering if he'd been able to get to a hospital, if there'd been one nearer the reserve—but that wouldn't have helped. That poison works very fast, usually. The fact is, he shouldn't have been here at all, wasting his time. If he'd stayed in the States, caring for ladies' poodles, he'd still be alive." He leaned forward, putting his glass on the low table. "Don't look at me that way, because there's no point in our getting into another power-struggle argument about things we don't agree on."

No, he was quite right; there wasn't. "Your doctor friend," Jenny asked coolly, "Dr. Du Mond—have you been friends for a long time?"

"Since medical school at the Sorbonne. We got drunk

together in Paris the night we learned we'd both passed, and ran into some good-looking American nurses who were touring the Left Bank. Paul asked Heller out and she hasn't seen Kansas City since." He picked up the decanter. "More wine?"

"No, thank you. What would he have done with his life, do you think, if he hadn't come here to practice? Surely there must have been many choices."

"Paul? Mmm—let me think. Well, his father is a plastic surgeon in Paris, makes a stultifying amount of money doing film stars' faces. Paul could have gone into practice with him, I imagine. Of course, he never wanted to."

"And why didn't he?" She leaned forward a little, enjoying getting through the shell Damien had around himself much of the time, in spite of the charm and polished manners.

He was silent for a few seconds. "I suppose," he said finally, "because he wanted to do something important."

"And you, Damien? Did you feel that way too, when you first came here?"

His eyes didn't waver. "I came here to get away from the woman I was married to at the time. Getting lost in the jungle may seem a rather unique way of making the best of a bad situation, but in my case, it was the one place I felt Pamela wouldn't follow and try to drag me back to Cape Hampton. That's a very rich, very snotty little town just north of New York, where her father owns the bank and a lot of the shopping centers. I had a practice going there; my kids went to private schools and Pam and I had a lot of credit cards. The great American dream." A kind of bitter quality had crept into his voice. "I got letters from Paul, telling me about life here. He talked about the bush and the rain forest and the way things looked on a quiet morning, very early. I didn't come, at first, because I didn't—I didn't want to leave my kids. When I did go, I gave Pam an

91

option—either she let me have custody or I'd get it on my own terms. What happened was that she showed up with the children. I hadn't counted on that."

He had said her name—Pamela. His past suddenly changed things; it was as if such a strong involvement with someone else put a kind of shadow between them.

"And your wife—didn't care for Africa?"

"She hated it, loathed it, every minute and second. Her father kept sending her poison-pen letters about how I'd ruined her otherwise dandy life, and from her point of view, I suppose I did. It takes a very special kind of woman to live here, day in, day out. The life style can be ruthless." He stood up abruptly, as if the conversation were ended. "Come on—I'll show you Heller's greenhouse. She says she raises orchids instead of kids."

She followed him down some open steps in the back, a narrow stairway that led into a private walled garden. Here, a pit had been dug in the ground for the roasting of meat; plants had been placed carefully along the stone wall, and there was a small, carved birdbath near the gate. The entire effect was one of tranquility and order, as if Heller spent a lot of time working out here.

The greenhouse was at the far end of the yard, a small, green-glassed room with the most amazing flowers growing there—huge orchids, some a pale lavender blending into a deep purple; some cream-colored blending into a pink or peach shade—all of them huge, exquisitely lovely.

"I've never seen anything like them," Jennifer said, bending over a huge flowering white orchid plant. "They're so beautiful they seem unreal!"

"A lot of life is like that." Damien's voice was surprisingly serious. "Too beautiful to be real. Did you know that those plants bloom just once a year, and when the flower is finished, the plant itself is very ugly? Look at that stalk—would you ever think anything as beautiful as an orchid could come from that?"

"I suppose everything is beautiful at some time or another in its life," she said gently. He looked so—*unhappy*. That was the only word for it; she looked at him as he stood there by the doorway, like some kind of stranger in this moistly warm world of blooming, beautiful flowers. "You don't care for flowers, Damien?"

"Not as much as I used to. Ready to go?" He didn't wait for her, but instead, turned and stood outside. She took one last look at those beautiful, potted plants and then closed the greenhouse door behind her.

"Why did you show that to me? That place—it upsets you, doesn't it, Damien?"

He walked protectively close to her in the slanting rain. "I always stop in when I'm here. Those flowers are Heller's pride and joy."

Their host was waiting for them in the large room where now there were no waiting patients. Paul Du Mond was smiling, still wearing his white med jacket, but he held a cup of coffee in one hand and poured brimming cups for Damien and Jennifer. They had a glimpse of Heller, busy out in the kitchen.

"So you've come from the States, Miss Logan. I imagine you're still in a state of shock; am I right?"

"Shock, Dr. Du Mond?"

He smiled. He was a handsome man, with a certain weariness around his eyes. There was something in his manner toward Damien, a certain tone he used, that she couldn't decipher. For now, she settled into one of the large, very soft chairs and sipped the coffee.

"Of course—it happens to everyone who comes over here. First, you find the animals delightfully amusing, then you find the heat or the flies or the rain not very amusing, and then, when you've been here for a while, the crucial time comes." He seemed to be teasing, yet there was that note of seriousness in his voice. "The time when one must decide to go or to stay. I hope you, Miss Logan, will decide to stay on. It's very refreshing to see my friend Damien with someone like you."

"Thank you." What, Jennifer wondered, was their secret; what was the mystery that seemed to exist between these two men? One could easily sense the camaraderie between them, but there was something else—unspoken. Whatever it was, Heller, Jenny sensed, knew about it too. She, like her husband, was perhaps a shade too teasing, and during dinner, both Heller and Paul kept talking about the shortage of doctors, the expected rash of yearly illnesses that the heavy damp rains caused, the babies that would be born in the bush unattended.

The meal, served in a dining room overlooking the street, was simple but delicious. Heller had utilized ingredients she had bought at the local street market—rice, chicken and the staple, couscous with big, plump raisins all through it. The talk drifted from the weather to the need for a regular clinic and hospital closer than the one here in the city.

"You're just trying to get patients out of your living room," Damien said, his voice joking, but still with that odd restraint to it. "My compliments on the wine, Paul."

"A gift from one of my patients. Makes it himself. By the way, this is the chap with the toes missing; I told you about him last time you were here. I'd like to discuss the prognosis with you for a while after dinner."

Something had leaped into Damien's blue eyes. "The man who got caught in the snare—yes; I remember your telling me."

After dinner was finished, the two men remained at the table; Heller had cleared it, bringing more coffee and a decanter of brandy.

"I really don't need help with the dishes," she told Jenny. "Someone comes in every day, and if there's nothing to do, she stands on the balcony and flirts with men down in the street. We'd best leave her something to keep her busy." She smiled at Jennifer, this slight, calm little woman who seemed perfectly contented living here in the midst of a teeming, sometimes violent city so far from home. "Why don't we go and have a look at my babies? My flowers, that is. I grow—"

"Orchids," Jennifer said. "I know; Damien showed me. I was very impressed."

Heller, who had been reaching for a heavy raincoat from a peg in the kitchen, seemed to pause. "Damien took you out there? That's strange." She shoved her thin arms into the coat. "He hasn't been out there for years."

"I thought he was a regular visitor. He seemed to know a lot about them."

They were outside now, hurrying through the rain and early darkness. Heller held open the greenhouse door and once again, Jennifer stepped inside to a quiet, moist world where every inch of space held a blooming or near-blooming orchid plant.

This time, she stayed much longer, walking up and down the earth-floor aisles with Heller, while Heller explained about the plants, pointing out the ones with buds, the ones whose flowers were fading.

"I suppose it might seem strange to you, the way I treat my plants as if they're people," Heller said, poking a small drainage tube inside a clay pot. "In a way, it's what I like to think of as my controlled world. In here, if I nourish my flowers and feed them certain things and keep them well watered, chances are about ninety-five to one they'll bloom for me. But with people, it's different." She turned to look at Jenny. "I'm a nurse, but I've never been able to get used to seeing people die. And a lot of people die here, when there's really no need. We need a clinic closer to the bush country, and we need one badly. My husband is a brilliant doctor, but even he can't save someone who needs help in a hurry and has to come all the way into the city to get it."

Jennifer paused over the head of a lilac-colored, nodding orchid.

"Does this have something to do with Damien, Heller?"

Heller's eyes deepened. "How much do you know about him?"

"Why—very little, actually."

"Your aunt hasn't told you anything about him at all?" There seemed to be a certain urgency in Heller's tone.

"No," Jenny said slowly. "Aunt Maggie hates gossip. Heller—what is it about him that everyone seems to know but me?"

Heller had bent her head over a flower; when she straightened up, she looked vastly uncomfortable, as if some unwanted task had been thrust upon her.

"Well," she said quietly, "you're bound to find out sooner or later."

"If you feel I ought to know that Damien has been married," Jenny said somewhat uncomfortably, "yes; I know that."

"Is that all he told you about his marriage?"

"Heller, I really don't think it's any of my business. Please—"

"Okay then." Heller put a watering can high on a shelf and dusted off her hands on a handy rag. "Come on, I've got some very good sweets you can take back to the kids at your aunt's place."

"You don't think I'm being rude?"

"Of course not. It's very nice of you not to want to pry. However, if the two of you are going to go on, shall we say, I hope Damien has a nice, long talk with you."

Suddenly, Jenny felt as if she wanted to run, to get out of there, away from that enclosed, warm little place with its boxed-in beauty, away from this very nice, sensible lady who seemed to want very much to talk about Damien's past. Somehow, his past frightened Jenny. To know about it would be like opening a door on something she had no right to see.

"Dr. Lear and I haven't got a romance going," Jenny said, her voice low. "It—it's nothing like that. I especially wanted to see him again because I've got a rather wild idea concerning the children and I wanted to bounce it off someone. Not only that—he can help me make it possible."

"You're wasting your time," Heller said dryly. "Look, the truth is, he doesn't think anybody should stay here. He thinks people should pack up and get as far away from here as possible. He wants to leave it to the hoot owls and jackals."

"And yet, he stays." Jenny looked through the rain, to the Du Monds' brightly lit apartment. She could make out the forms of the two men, sitting at the table, talking. A kind of fierce yearning flooded over her, so electric that it startled her. *Why,* she thought, *I'm falling in love with him, reacting like a stupid schoolgirl at the very sight of him! Am I so starved for love, so desperate for affection that I'd let myself tumble again, this soon after my last near-fatal mistake?*

Surely not. Very quickly, she buttoned her raincoat, ducked her head and hurried across the dark expanse of grass leading to the apartment's open back stairway.

"There you are," Damien said from the dining room, getting up. "Did Heller give away any of her secrets?"

"No," Jennifer said quickly, perhaps too quickly. "She—she's very close about her lovely orchids. She wouldn't tell me a thing."

But everyone in that room knew what she was really saying: *Don't worry, Dr. Lear; if you want me to know your secret, you're going to have to tell me yourself, because neither my aunt nor your good friend Heller seems to want it to wait much longer!*

And if he didn't—it really didn't matter, did it? Since he

wouldn't help her with her plan to bring the children around to a totally new way of thinking about the bush, she probably wouldn't be seeing him again anyway.

Or so she thought.

SIX

By the time they left Nairobi, the rain had slackened somewhat, so that it was only a light spattering against the windows of Damien's truck.

"You liked them, didn't you?" His voice was warm in the close darkness.

"Of course. They're lovely, dedicated people."

"Kindly stop sounding like a travel folder. What did you really think of them?" He made a sharp turn off the road; they bounced along in silence for a while. Jenny didn't remember having come this way on their trip in.

"I think there's—something lacking. Something wrong. Not wrong enough to keep them from loving each other, but wrong, all the same."

Now it was his turn to be silent for a moment. Finally, he pulled into a clearing, light-streaked, silent, somehow lonely.

"You're a very astute girl. Yes," he said, "something is missing. But you know what they say about best-laid plans of mice and men."

"She wanted to tell me something," Jenny said softly. "But she didn't. She said—she also said that you wouldn't help me help the children."

He let his breath out. "I won't be party to some goody-two-shoes fool plan to make the kids love all the nice lions, because it won't work."

"It might. All I'm asking," Jenny said quickly, "is that

you furnish transportation. I don't mean just for picnics in the rain forest. I mean taking them into towns where they have hides and animal ivory for sale. They need to be told that there aren't going to be any more animals if poaching doesn't stop. They need to be taught the—the history of wildlife and then maybe they'll respect it."

He looked at her in the half-darkness of the truck cab. "What about your precious reserves? Are you going to teach them that's the only way to save Africa?" Suddenly, he reached over her and opened the door. "Get out," he said. "I want to show you something."

He came around the truck and took her hand, walking with her on the firm, wet ground; the wet grass clung to her ankles.

"Now," Damien said, pointing, "this is elephant country, or used to be. People, well-meaning people like your aunt and uncle, have confined thousands of them to unnatural boundaries, sanctified ghettos, a lot of them, and what nobody seems to want to admit is that the animal population increases beyond the limits of food supply. Believe it or not," he said, his voice low, "this used to be a food base, a forest. Then, it became grassland. Next, it'll be desert, where nothing grows and nothing feeds."

"You never have anything good to say about my aunt and uncle's work, do you?" But seeing that vast expanse of seeming wasteland, her heart had begun beating in something close to shame. "I can't believe their work isn't helping animals," she said finally.

"Helping them exterminate themselves, that's what it's doing. You've heard, I suppose, of that place where elephants go to die?"

"Of course. But I don't see—"

"A lot of us," Damien told her, "happen to believe that place is none other than one of your precious game preserves. Come on; I'll drive you home."

* * *

It had not been a totally satisfying evening, although she found that, once in bed, she could not stop thinking about the events of the evening—the Du Monds, their rather cramped quarters, their seeming longing for something they didn't have, something they felt was essential. . . .

Suddenly, Jennifer sat up in bed, eyes wide. The rain outside made its steady, hissing sound and from somewhere in the house, a clock chimed.

It's Damien, she thought clearly. *That's what the problem is—he's what the problem is! They want him to go back into practice, along with them!*

She did not know if it was because of that, or because she feared her own feelings concerning him that made her decide not to like him, not to like him at all, to be totally on her aunt's side and never set foot anywhere near his lodge again.

Finally, she slept, hoping she would not again dream of herself in that emerald garden, the rain forest, in his arms.

She did not. In fact, she did not dream at all, and when Manguana came in with morning tea, Jenny felt tired still.

"You have company downstairs, Missy. Your aunt says to hurry up."

"Company? Do—is it Dr. Lear?" She was suddenly wide awake; all her resolutions about him seemed to have vanished and here she was, eager to see him again! .

"Only his truck. And three jeeps. And drivers. And a letter from the doctor. If you want hot bread, it is being baked in the kitchen."

"Did you say—his truck?" Quickly, Jenny went to the window, shoved it up and stuck her head out into the rainy day. There outside, in the driveway, was the big truck she had ridden in the evening before with Damien, plus, as Manguana had said, three jeeps. The drivers were nowhere to be seen; they were very likely having honey and bread in the kitchen.

"You want me to bring his note up to you?"

"No, thank you," Jenny said, turning from the window. "I'll be right down."

Downstairs, she found Maggie on the porch, feeding the roosting birds. One of them, a macaw named Father Pierre, clung to her wrist as she moved about the porch.

"Good morning, Jenny. We're going to need a soft-drink bottle with a nipple on it for that new baby zebra. Be sure to pick some up when you go into Nairobi today." She looked hard at Jenny. "I assume you *are* going in."

"Aunt Maggie, I can explain everything."

"No need, my dear. Obviously, you charmed Damien Lear to the point where he is laying his treasures at your feet. I've never seen anybody drive that truck but him. I guess one could say that settles the question."

"Aunt Maggie, I only asked him to provide transportation so that I could take some of the children into the city. I—I've had an idea swirling around in my head that has to do with poaching. . . ." Suddenly, she felt almost ashamed. "I know it must seem as if I'm forward and arrogant, coming here and wanting to change things. But please, even if it doesn't work, the children will enjoy the ride, I'm sure."

"Nothing good can come of any dealings of any kind with Damien Lear," Maggie said darkly, turning back to the birds. "Be sure the nipple fits tight on the bottle and while you're there, you might as well load some sugar cane in the back of that truck and bring it back too."

"Aren't you afraid we'll all be contaminated, Aunt Maggie?"

"Jenny!"

Jenny let her breath out. "I'm sorry—I didn't mean to be rude. I'd better start gathering up the children so we can get started."

But she hadn't reckoned with any of the problems that she would have to deal with, just to take four carloads of children into Nairobi.

While she was fixing lunches to take alone, she read the brief note from Damien, which had been carried by one of the drivers:

> *Stop in the café where we went last night. A hot meal will be waiting for you and the kids. The drivers have been instructed not to make any stops on the way due to poachers. It won't work, Jenny, but give it a good try. At least the kids will get to have a nice outing.*

How dare he say her plan wouldn't work!

But she found, finally, that she would only need one jeep and the truck; there simply weren't enough children allowed to go. Most of the parents who worked for Maggie were off someplace doing chores or tending to the animals, and the well-behaved youngsters would never leave unless given permission. So in the beginning, there was only one little girl and finally, her younger sister, then four from the village, grandchildren of Massukuntna and Manguana, piled into the jeep. So off they went, Jenny, the two drivers, neither of whom spoke any English at all, and the half-dozen children.

All along the way, the vicious wire nooses were in plain sight; the poachers had made no attempt at all to conceal them. They gaped between bushes and across trails; none contained living animals, Jenny was relieved to see, but one held a carcass, an impala, largely devoured by scavengers. She felt her stomach lurch at the sight.

"Chimungu," the children beside her began chanting, pointing to one of the huge black birds circling overhead. "Boss bird," one of them said, his voice matter-of-fact. "First he comes and then the vultures. First, he eats the eyeball."

"Tongo, kindly don't talk about it, okay?"

The boy grinned. "Okay."

"Oh-kay," said one of the little girls. And then they were all chanting the word, making it into a little song.

Strange, the sight of that poor dead animal hadn't bothered them one bit. They drove on, while above them, in the clouded, gray sky, the vultures wheeled and waited.

The sudden gift of transportation from Damien had come so suddenly and unexpectedly that Jennifer wasn't quite sure where to begin on her personal campaign to help stop the poaching. To talk to the children was going to be difficult; some of them understood and spoke no English at all, except for their favorite word: *okay*.

In Nairobi, over hot tea and a very sturdy meal of baked fish and peanut dressing, she remembered the painting she had wanted to do. *That's it*, she told herself, wiping the chin of a little girl who had spilled her tea, *I'll buy paints and plenty of poster paper and teach the children through drawings!*

It seemed like a splendid idea. She ended up buying not only poster paper and paints but canvas as well, finely grained, shipped from London. Then, holding the two littlest children by the hand, she set off for the nearest store with teeth, tusks, and skins for sale in the window.

The children stopped when Jennifer did; some of them pressed their little faces admiringly against the pane of window, peering inside at the gleaming animal teeth strung on a necklace of cowhide. For a brief, fleeting second, Jenny felt a kind of despair wash over her. They were so small and innocent; they saw absolutely nothing cruel or wrong about the horrible traps, the painful wounds of animals caught in those traps, the selling of the animals' parts for money. They had seen, after all, their fathers and uncles and probably their older brothers, to say nothing of their grandfathers—set traps and calmly extract wounded or dead animals from them, to be skinned, declawed and de-toothed, and ultimately sold. Why should they feel any differently?

Then, looking down into the liquid dark eyes of one of the little girls, Jennifer suddenly hugged her, hugged them all in a sweeping gesture, then she sat on the curb in front of the store, where rainwater in huge droplets fell from the covering awning and made small pools, and she began to draw.

The children were fascinated. First, she painted a sign on a large piece of posterboard that said in English: *Protectors of Tomorrow*. Since the children seemed delighted with the bright red coloring, the pretty letters they couldn't read, and the nice way Jenny went about doing it, with a kind of flourish, they all wanted to try their hand at it. At that point, they went back to the café, and wih more tea in front of them, they were each given a piece of posterboard and crayons.

"Elephant," Jenny told one little girl. She fashioned a trunk for herself with one arm and the children laughed delightedly, in unison. "Draw an elephant for me, Katula. Understand?"

They did; they all did, surprisingly swiftly. Twice, the words had to be translated for them by Damien's friend, the café's owner, but then, they all got down to work, heads bent over their drawings.

The final results were simply astounding.

Jenny looked at them once, twice, three times and then again, the last time with tears in her eyes. Three of them had drawn animals caught in traps. One of them, when asked to draw a bird, any bird, had chosen the *chimungu*, the "boss bird" they had seen on the trip down. The bird looked satiny black and beautiful; its tilting wings shone much like their own skin.

Clearly, they saw no evil at all in the killing of wild animals. The same quiet acceptance of life that allowed the children to assist in the birth of babies told them that animal killing and skin selling was a fact of life, much the same as the work of a boss bird was.

They ended the trip with a visit to the shop with the long awning in front. There, they quietly stood staring into showcases filled with small stuffed animals, elephant teeth, jewelry made from ivory, and handbags and suitcases covered with the stunningly beautiful skin of the cheetah.

They sang songs on the way back, sharing the boxed lunches Manguana had prepared for them. The rain had slackened somewhat; they passed within a hundred yards or so of the road leading to Damien's lodge, and quite suddenly, on impulse, she turned to the driver and tapped him on the shoulder.

"Will you take us to Dr. Lear's house, please?"

He looked a bit startled. She had forgotten he spoke no English.

"Dr. Lear's," Jenny said again, pointing toward the lodge. "That way!"

The driver stopped the truck and in turn, the jeep behind them stopped. Both drivers got out and, standing in the rain, had a conversation Jenny could not understand, except that twice they said Damien's name.

Then they climbed inside again and started the vehicles. The children squealed in delight and awe when they saw the porch of the lodge, with its elegant furniture, exquisite screens and flowers, and people wearing western clothes sitting there viewing the world.

"Come on," Jenny said briskly, once they'd stopped in front of the sprawling lodge. "That's right, bring your drawings. Don't step on them now—come on, out of the truck, kids."

And so they went, the six little ones, from the tallest, most dignified black boy to the tiniest, shyest little girl, who clung securely to Jenny's hand, across the wide lobby, past the staring, amused patrons who sat at the long bar or else

105

lounged in soft easy chairs, straight to the forbiddingly closed door of Damien Lear's office.

Jennifer knocked firmly but quietly, twice. Then, she found herself looking up into the startled blue eyes of Damien, who seemed to be looking at the children as if they were some rare breed.

"I'm afraid there's been a mistake," he said finally, his voice just on the edge of coolness. "The loan of the jeeps and truck didn't mean my guests can be—disturbed."

His words stung like a slap; they were totally unexpected and, it seemed to her, uncalled for. The boy who spoke English looked at Jenny uneasily.

"I—I thought you'd—the children did some drawings, of—of animals and I thought you might like to have them," she told him in a quiet little voice. "It's a sort of—payment for your kindness in lending us the jeep and truck."

Something, some fleeting look that held deep longing, came into his eyes, it seemed to her, as she held out the children's drawings.

"Thank you. I'll send them along to Heller; I daresay she'll do something clever in the way of decorating the waiting room there with them. I trust you had a very stimulating day?"

"Very. And thank you," Jennifer said evenly, "for the meal at the café. I'm sure the children would thank you too but some of them don't speak English."

"My pleasure, Miss Logan. And now, if you and your little friends will excuse me—"

"Damien—"

Cold eyes regarded her as if they were strangers. "Yes?"

"What—what is it? I thought you'd be pleased to see us—that is, I thought, when you sent the truck and jeeps, you'd become interested in what I'm trying to do."

"I sent the jeeps and truck to take a crowd of very nice kids to the city for lunch," he told her unflinchingly. "Whatever else happened is none of my concern. However,

I do have a house rule here: no children allowed as guests or as visitors. I told you before, this isn't a place for children."

"I apologize if we contaminated your million-dollar establishment, Doctor."

There was a second or two of silence between them. For the life of her, she could not understand his seemingly sudden swings in mood; one moment he seemed generous to a fault, wanting to help her by giving jeeps and a free meal to the children, and the next, he was practically throwing them off the premises!

"We'll go back in the truck if you don't mind," Jenny said finally, nearly asking for the drawings back, then thinking better of it. "We can all crowd in there easier than the jeep. Unless, of course, you're afraid the children might get it sticky. I understand the truck is one thing you're truly fond of."

A small smile touched his lips. "Obviously, Miss Logan, you haven't heard about some of my lady guests."

She could not recall, later, having walked back through the lobby, past the grinning, overdressed, overfed guests, back to the waiting truck with the children. On the trip back to the reserve, she carefully looked out the window, holding a sleeping little girl in her arms.

It was only when the children sat quietly and tiredly in the kitchen, at the long table with Massukuntna at the head of it, telling him stories about their happy day, that Jennifer finally allowed herself to assess what had happened. Manguana was too busy in the kitchen, apparently, to have lit the rush lamps, and her Aunt Maggie was nowhere to be seen. In the twilight, the big, sprawling house seemed somehow to become a part of land, like a bird's nest or a refuge made by the animals. It smelled vaguely of flowers and jungle lime; the only sounds were the soft murmur of the children's voices and the ticking of Maggie's big old clock, a nine-day wind, coming from the adjoining room.

On the porch, Jenny leaned against one of the posts and thought of him.

It was almost as if she dared herself to, promising some inner self that this time, there would be no possibility of inflicted pain, since she was immune to all of that now. She liked to think she had passed far beyond the capacity for that kind of hurt; after Brendon, she'd made her mind up never to put herself in such a vulnerable position again.

But Damien's words had stung, hurt her; his coldness had somehow chilled her heart, so that she wanted not to strike back at him in any way but instead to withdraw, to leave, to—hide. *Hide.* An ugly word, and yet, she reminded herself, wasn't that just what she'd done by coming here? The truth was, she'd run as fast as she could from anything that might remind her of what had nearly happened with Brendon.

"Hello," Maggie said suddenly, coming in from the side door. She wore a long raincoat with a hood. Her glasses were fogged and had slipped down her nose a bit. "I saw the truck ambling by a moment ago, so I suspected you were back. All intact, I hope?"

"Everybody is fine," Jenny told her. "I think they're all in the kitchen."

Maggie was taking off her coat, watching Jennifer. "Well," she said, her tone hearty, "do you want to talk about it?"

"I don't know what you mean."

"None of that, Jenny. What did he do this time to upset you?"

"Nothing. I mean, nothing that I shouldn't have known would happen."

Maggie smoothed back her auburn hair; there was bird seed in it from the evening's feeding. "To tell you the truth, I was amazed that he sent the jeeps and truck around. Since it had to do with children, I rather imagined he'd flatly refuse to help you in any way."

"Aunt Maggie, why does he seem to—to dislike children so?"

Quite suddenly, Maggie's attitude had changed. She always seemed to be very open and candid with Jennifer; now, however, she seemed markedly vague.

"I wouldn't say he dislikes them, Jennifer. There's nothing he's done to indicate that. He simply doesn't like to see them growing up around here."

"What does he advocate? That nobody have babies?"

"He'd probably like that, I'm sure. Then, according to Damien, we could all pack up and go home or someplace and let the animals take over what is rightfully theirs. Would you like a nightcap, Jenny?"

"No, thank you. Aunt Maggie, you aren't going to tell me, are you?"

Maggie had started toward the fragrant aroma coming from the kitchen. At the doorway, she turned once again to look at Jennifer.

"Tell you what, dear?"

"Why Damien is so uncomfortable around children. It—it seems very strange," Jenny said, "for a doctor—"

Suddenly, she stopped talking. She and her aunt looked at each other across the room.

"Aunt Maggie—" Her voice trembled in the stillness. "Damien's patient, the one he—lost. Was it—was it a child?"

Maggie's eyes didn't change or waver. "I told you, Jennifer, I detest gossip, and it seems to me that your question comes easily under that heading. If Damien Lear wants to let you in on his life's business, I'm sure he will."

"And in the meantime, I'm free to think whatever I want. Aunt Maggie, don't you think it would be kinder of you to tell me the truth?"

"Kinder? Perhaps," Maggie softly. "But certainly not wiser. Damien himself would tell you that here in the jungle, we don't always do the kindest thing—but we try to do the wisest."

Her work had piled up on the small desk near the porch; Jennifer, having taken a brief bath in the darkness of the shower stall, while a wild bird hooted at her nakedness, had wrapped herself in a snug robe and, in the flickering light from the rush lamps, was busily typing up letters for Maggie.

Her aunt had said goodnight hours before; the children had been taken to their homes by parents, except for the ones who lived in the house with Maggie, along with their young mother, and now, it was a silent, fragrant world that Jenny felt herself a part of as she sat at her work.

But her fingers missed the proper keys and she made so many mistakes that finally, leaning back in the chair, she gave it up. No use to keep on trying to think about budget figures to be sent to the central committee; Damien had spoiled her thinking for the night, anyway. Perhaps tomorrow, when the children were around the house and Maggie was up and about and the birds were yelling for breakfast and the new day had begun in earnest, she would feel differently.

Now, all she felt was a sort of burning hurt, pain not physical and yet it was surely pain. Why had he been so downright rude and nasty, when she'd been filled with all sorts of warm feelings, when she had wanted him to applaud the children's paintings and perhaps even admit that she may have made some small beginning in the changing of their thinking about animals?

Because he doesn't care, idiot, that's why! Because he doesn't care about what happens to people here, or animals here. All he really cares about is running that super-swank lodge of his, his ivory tower, where he's a sort of god, and he can sit there in his fancy, air-conditioned office and announce to everybody that he loathes the jungle, hates the

110

country and only stays because rich fools pay him a lot of money to go off and shoot animals!

She got up from the small desk and walked onto the porch. In some odd way, she wished she could hear music coming from the lodge; she could be angry then. But Damien had complied politely with her aunt's order that he stop bothering them with sounds in the night, and now, there was only an oppressive silence around Maggie's house.

Why should she care so much?

Sometime in the night, she thought she heard the sound of a motor, but she turned over, shut her eyes, and ignored it. Tomorrow was going to be an important day. It was time to explain to her aunt what she hoped to do. With Maggie's support, there was no telling what might happen!

She woke up to the lovely aroma of Manguana's coffee. Stretching, Jenny turned her head to the window, seeing the endless rain; she got out of bed and, for some reason, looked out the window.

That was when she saw the truck, Damien's truck, plus the jeeps—four of them. All five drivers were eating breakfast they'd apparently brought from the lodge. Her heart began beating harder—he had sent the vehicles for her to use again, for the children to use again! She certainly hadn't expected this.

Maggie, glasses slipped to her nose, peered over them at Jennifer, who was busy eating her grapefruit and making notes on a small notebook.

"Are you by any chance writing Dr. Lear a poison pen letter, dear?"

Jenny looked up, her face coloring a bit. "Of course not. I'm not writing to him at all—there's no reason to."

"What about his truck out there? Pass the brown sugar, dear, please."

"What about it?" Jenny put down her pencil, taking a small breath. "Aunt Maggie, if he wants to loan us the

111

transportation, I'm going to take it. Otherwise, I'd have to worry about how to get all the kids into Nairobi again today."

Maggie gave her a long, level look. "Jennifer," she said finally, gently putting down her spoon, "I think it's about time we talk. Now don't start looking nervous, dear; I'm only going to ask you to kindly explain why you feel the sudden need to round up as many children as you can find and take them to the city again today." Her gaze was steady. "And more than that, why you allow Damien Lear to infringe upon our work and our life here by having property owned by him parked in front of my house!"

"Aunt Maggie," Jenny said carefully, quietly, "I—I know how you feel about Damien. And more and more, I'm finding myself agreeing with you. He *is* rude; he *is* ruthless; he really doesn't seem to care much about the people here or the animals. A little, perhaps, but not much. He certainly isn't dedicated to anything, except maybe the making of a lot of money."

"Go on, Jennifer. What else about the man do you find so repulsive that you feel you must still keep in touch with him?"

There was a silence. "It isn't that," Jenny said finally. "Honestly, it isn't. It's that I've got a plan that concerns the children and it's going to work, Aunt Maggie; I can feel it working."

"*Feel* it working?"

Jenny nodded. "Yesterday, the way the children behaved, the way they loved being together and with me. The paintings they did—they were just so—thoughtful and—and detailed—"

"Paintings?"

"I bought them some supplies in Nairobi, pencils and paints and posterboard. I had no idea they would do such beautiful work! You see, they probably know more about animals than they realize. It's just that someone needs to—

to put them in tune with—with feeling differently about them, that's all."

"That," Maggie said dryly, going back to her breakfast, "will never happen, my dear. What we have in these children is the sum total of generations of people who depend upon killing animals, by poaching if necessary, so that they can survive. And you expect the children to suddenly want to make house pets of them all!"

Jennifer looked at her aunt. This was painful for her, for them both, but the moment had come to try to explain what she hoped to do. If Maggie didn't approve, then, Jenny had decided, she would simply have to decide whether or not she dared go ahead with a project without her aunt's help or even her consent.

"First of all," she said evenly, "I need to take some kind of crash course on wildlife. I plan to go to the library and send away and do anything that's needed, so that I'll know things like—how long is a giraffe's tongue and how much water can an elephant hold in his truck. Then, as the group of children begins to grow, I can teach them things they might not know, or if they do already know, they can teach me." She leaned forward, closer to her aunt. "The really important thing is that we'll be communicating to each other about the animals, learning new things about them, so that they won't just be meat and skins and teeth and tusks to be sold in shops for money!"

"In other words, you hope to wipe out everything they've learned about animals, turn them completely about and start anew." Maggie shook her head. "How do you know their parents will put up with that? What makes you think these people are going to allow their kids to spend much of their time sitting around measuring a giraffe's tongue?"

"Aunt Maggie, if only you'd not feel that it's a sort of mission impossible! For one thing, all children feel love for other living things; we need only tap that source and let it

113

spill over and then, they'll begin to care about the wildlife near them! I want to take them to shops and let them get angry because handbags are being sold there, made out of cheetah skin; I want them to be furious when they see animals' teeth strung as beads—"

"I see. And while you're changing the face of this part of the world, what is Damien doing? What, Jennifer? Helping you out with jeeps and a nice truck, maybe sending along food for the children's lunch—what?" Her voice was quite cold. "Let me tell you something, my dear. No matter how hard you try to get that man interested in your project, it won't work. Damien Lear is beyond caring. He's dead inside, Jenny, just as surely as if that fever had taken him too!" Suddenly, her face went pale. "I've said too much. If you're going into Nairobi with the children, tell Manguana to pack lunches—if Damien Lear hasn't already sent along food."

"Aunt Maggie—" Jenny's voice was low; her heart had begun that slow, heavy beating again, the way it did when some new truth about Damien suddenly became clear. "What did you mean when you said the fever—"

"I told you; I've said too much. Excuse me now, Jennifer, I've got correspondence to take care of. It seems my new helper has been spending a lot of her time driving around in a borrowed truck!"

"I'll do it tonight, I promise!" But the words she wanted to say, the questions she wanted to ask, she held back. Even when she made the arrangements to once again take the children into the city, her mind seemed to be spinning, reeling with questions. Maggie had said something about a fever—how had she put it? That fever, something about a fever that might have taken him too. What fever? And who was taken, while Damien was left behind? Dead inside, her aunt had said. Was he? Could it possibly be that a man who smiled and spoke and almost kissed a woman could be so full of agony inside his heart, his spirit, that he could be referred to as "dead"?

This time, there were enough children to fill the truck and the waiting jeeps too. They began their procession shortly before ten, heading once again for Nairobi, where, the driver had said through his ten-year-old interpreter, lunch would be served for all the children; Dr. Lear would take care of the bill.

On the drive there, past the gleaming wet rain forest, past the heavy bush country that strung itself around the winding lake, Jennifer's mind refused to leave Damien. She saw, in her mind's eye, his blue eyes, warming only briefly when he looked at her, deepening with some feeling the time they nearly kissed, clouding when she tried to talk about his past, and finally, cold as winter, frosty, steel-blue, the time she gave him the children's little drawings.

They spent hours in the library that day, while Jenny pored over books on African wildlife, trying to remember each species, trying to put down facts in her mind that she could repeat to the children.

She got a lot of help from the librarian, a pretty girl who had, she told Jenny, studied library science in London but had decided to come back home to work. The children were behaving very well that day; they sat like small angels, heads bowed over books about animals. More and more, Jenny was beginning to understand that there were many, many other people besides herself who felt as she did in this country, people who wanted permanent protection for some of the endangered animals. There were certain types of monkeys who were once plentiful but who were now nearly extinct; at one time, the soft-spoken librarian explained, monkey-fur coats were considered very fashionable. Not only that, many of the cute, tiny little monkeys had been snatched away from their mothers' breasts and hauled off in crates to other countries, badly cared for on the way over and very often dead when they finally got there.

It was, of course, heart-breaking, but new, strict laws had done away with a lot of that.

"Oh," the girl said suddenly, looking up from one of the books she'd just handed Jenny, "I nearly forgot—there's a message here for you, from Dr. Damien Lear."

Jenny's heart lightened. "Dr. Lear left a message?"

"Yes. He said to tell you to stop by the same café for picnic-box lunches to take to the rain forest today."

"Thank you," Jenny said, hoping disappointment didn't show in her voice.

They picked up the box lunches, however, then she herded the children back into the truck and jeeps and along with their drivers, they headed for the vast rain forest. Once there, Jenny felt a strange sense of peace coming over her; it was almost as if she could leave her anger with Damien, her feelings of alternate dislike and deep attraction behind her and here, in this mysterious place, allow herself to remember only the feelings she'd had when they had been so close, when he had made her feel the way every woman yearns to feel, the way Manguana's man had been able to make her feel all these years—*beloved*.

Still, she had to admit that what she proposed to do might well seem impossible. There were moments when it seemed that way to her, too. She really knew so little about what she wanted to teach. Could she ever cram her head full of enough facts to tell the children?

A feeling of defeat had begun to creep over her, although she tried to push it down. There were capped cups filled with comforting tea; she sat on the forest floor and ate and drank with the children, the sense of doubt spoiling what should have been a very nice picnic.

She told them about giraffes and even took a yardstick out of her bookbag to show them how long fourteen inches was, the average length of the giraffe's tongue. She talked about how they got their food and was delighted when one little girl asked if they ever got a sore throat.

"Okay now, let's go on to elephants. Bama, how many gallons of water can an elephant hold in its trunk?"

"Two!"

"Right!" She smiled at them, feeling much better. "Tomorrow, I'm going to tell you about spoors and how to recognize them. And I wanted to compliment all of you on your drawings—"

A sudden, piercing scream broke the quiet. It came again and then again—a child's voice!

At once, the other children sprang up, eyes wide with fear. One of the drivers, who had been dozing in the truck, leaped out and came running toward Jennifer, who stood frozen in horror. *An animal,* she thought, *an animal is killing one of the children—*

The drivers were all pointing, running to the east, toward the narrow road. Jenny ran after them, not really knowing what she could do, but ready to do anything to help. There was a wide clearing on the far side of the trees, and there, although she couldn't see the child, she saw the drivers huddled around a small circle. Her heart began pounding in slow dread.

Then, getting closer, she saw that it was not an animal that had done harm to the child, but one of the wire mesh traps. Somehow, the little boy had wandered from the group and had gotten himself caught in one of the poachers' traps. He was very small; his little face was stained with tears, and when he saw Jenny, he held out his arms to her.

His leg was caught in the wire; bright blood spurted from the side of it. Behind Jenny, the other children stood in terrified little clusters.

"Too much blood, Missy," one of the drivers said in broken English. "Got to go to see Dr. Du Mond."

Jenny's mind was racing. They were miles out of Nairobi now; the drive was slow and arduous at best. It would take them perhaps thirty minutes or more to reach Paul and Heller's apartment, and by that time the child might well have lost more blood than he could stand losing. One of the drivers had carried the crying child to the truck; suddenly, Jenny turned to face the circle of drivers.

"We've no time to go back to the city. Drive to Dr. Lear's lodge as quickly as possible. The rest of you take the other children back to my aunt's."

It was, to say the least, a wild trip. The driver seemed intent on either getting them there in record time or killing them all on the way. Jenny, who held the bleeding child on her lap, crooning and whispering encouragement to him, thought at least twice they would surely go off the road and turn over. She held the little boy close to her, closed her eyes and silently prayed they would make it to the lodge without a wreck, that Damien would be there—*please God, let him be there*—and that the warm, sticky blood which had soaked through the makeshift bandage onto her skirt wouldn't mean that the child's life was draining away.

Finally, the truck spun from the narrow road onto a wider, paved one, leaving the dense jungle behind. This was another clearing; the lodge was in plain sight now. The driver skidded to a jolting stop right in front of the red-carpeted steps leading up to the porch; guests sitting there got up from lounge chairs to come and stare.

The driver helped Jenny out; she carried the bleeding child in her arms, and the driver sprinted ahead of her to hold open the door. Inside, the cold, air-conditioned air, scented with the aroma of expensive perfume and rich food, came at her. Two women sitting at the bar stared, faces going pale, as Jenny ran toward the closed door of Damien's office.

Then, the door opened and he stood there, Damien, shirt

sleeves rolled up over strong arms, eyes narrowing as he saw the child in her arms.

He came forward in three giant steps and gently took the boy from her.

SEVEN

"What the devil happened?"

Damien was bending over the child; he had spoken to the boy softly, kindly, placing him on the huge, polished desk, one strong hand on the child's chest.

"Snare got him, Doctor," the driver said, from somewhere behind Jenny.

"You know better than that," Damien told the boy, "but you'll be fine, so stop crying. Just let me have a good look, okay?" He leaned closer. "I can do a patch-up job here, but he'll have to go to the hospital."

The child began howling.

"Okay," Damien said, "okay, maybe I can do it here. It's surface, mostly, nothing vital touched. Do you know there is poison sometimes on the snares?"

The tearful little boy nodded miserably.

"And that you are very, very lucky to only have a nasty gash on your leg?"

The big eyes blinked.

"Good. Then I'll patch you up and we'll put you in a spare room for the night." His eyes met Jenny's. "Perhaps Miss Logan would like to keep you company."

It worked. The child grinned and nodded and suddenly Damien was giving quiet orders to everybody—the desk must be sterile; everybody must wash up, and where the devil was his bag; he hadn't used it for years and it was locked up someplace—

* * *

"Eight stitches," he said finally, and he smiled at the boy. "You did very well indeed. I think a nice supper and a present or two are in order." He lifted the child into his arms. "Tell you what—while you rest, I'll send word to your mother and you can be thinking about what you'd like for a present."

"Ice cream," Biano said promptly.

"Sure; we've got plenty of that. And we'll come up with something else."

Jenny, feeling slightly faint, leaned against the door.

"You okay, Miss Logan?"

She straightened up. "I'm fine, Doctor. I was just getting my second wind."

The room was actually a suite, probably the most expensive in the lodge. It consisted of a huge bedroom, with a low, king-sized bed covered with a lovely spread that looked like zebra skin but wasn't, Jenny saw with relief. There was an adjoining room, a living room with sleek, modern furniture, and a sweeping view of the jungle beyond.

The presents for Biano began coming about ten minutes later, mostly from guests. There was a jungle hat sent from Damien, too big, of course, but Biano wore it anyway, sitting up happily in the huge bed, eating the peach ice cream Jenny fed him from a silver spoon. Outside, it was beginning to get dark; a message had been sent to the boy's parents and to Maggie.

It looked as if Jenny would be spending the night there.

She wasn't sure just when it was it happened; she only knew that she woke up, there on the cot in the room with the sleeping child, and at once, she knew something had happened, something had changed. She sat up in the near-

120

darkness, wearing only her slip, and stared out the wide window.

There was a moon, and moonlight lay like a blue-silver pool on the polished floor. Strange, the moon was so clear, so lovely and bright, so much brighter than usual—

Then, she realized what it was. It had stopped raining!

It was odd, that new silence, a world without the heavy, constant beating of rain against glass, against wood and pavement, slanting, slashing, never ending. But it had ended; the night was clear and cloudless and, when Jenny unlocked and opened one of the windows, the air was rain-washed and fragrant, sweet with the scent of jungle moss and flowers, heady and somehow pure, as if a new beginning had been made.

When the knock came at the door, she wasn't surprised; it was as if she had only half-slept, lying close to the sleeping child for a while, to comfort him with the warmth of her body, then going to the cot to try to sleep through the night. But she had not slept well; she had dreamed of riding in Damien's truck, a mad, wild ride through tangled, soaked brush, an agonizingly slow trip to get help for the bleeding boy, and finally, Damien, Damien in her dream, lifting the child, bending over him with great kindness and tenderness, much the way it had actually happened.

The knock came again, quietly, but not secretly. She slipped into her clothes and opened the door.

"Did I wake you?" He wore pajamas and a robe; he was smiling at her.

"No. That is—I was in bed but the rain woke me up. I mean the lack of it."

"Didn't anybody tell you that it doesn't always rain in Africa?"

"No," she said, and she saw that he was teasing her. "I should have known the sun always shines, sooner or later."

"Very true, Miss Logan. Now, if you don't mind, I'd like to take a quick look at my unexpected patient."

Without waking the boy, Damien gently lifted the sterile bandage and addressed himself to the wound. Then, having quietly covered the child once again, he walked across the large room to the door. Jenny had stood behind him, glad he had come, that he had been concerned enough to come to the child at this time of night.

"Damien?" She looked at him as he started to leave. "I—I was wondering if—are you sleepy?"

"No," he told her. "As a matter of fact, I was just thinking of going for a drive. Care to join me?"

"But—will the boy—"

"He'll sleep until dawn with that sedative. The best way to celebrate the close of the rainy season is to go out and view the world at once, you know—before the nights begin to get very hot and steamy and you find yourself wishing it would rain again."

The truck was parked where the driver had left it, in front of the lodge. Jenny dressed and then waited on the porch while Damien went to change. When he reappeared, he wore the usual, faded slacks and a white shirt, sleeves rolled up. He started the truck, backed it out, and then they were speeding down the twisting, narrow road that led to the thick underbrush. Here, the trees were still bowed from months of heavy rain, but the moonlight was crystal clear, lighting the brush and forest like a huge spotlight. To their left lay Lake Victoria, calm and black, except where the moonlight spilled across its rippling surface.

Damien stopped the truck in a clearing near the lake.

"I want you to meet a friend of mine," he said. He got out of the truck, came around and opened the door on Jenny's side.

"A friend? Here?"

"He's a night prowler. Doesn't sleep when the rest of the herd does. Come on; don't be afraid. See that stretch of woods over there? He's eaten most of it himself, the old devil. He's particularly fond of acacias."

He took her hand, leading her off the road into the bush. Now Jenny could hear sounds, the night sounds of the jungle. From high above, shining eyes watched her; she looked up and cried out in fright.

"It's only a lioness," Damien told her calmly. "She won't jump you—not unless you try to hurt her cubs. Come on, old Max is probably around here somewhere, having a late snack."

She stayed very close to the comforting presence of Damien as he led her deeper into the bush, using a powerful flashlight to guide them. Then, very suddenly, he stopped walking, turning off the light.

"Hear that? That's got to be old Max."

"You must know him very well," Jenny said nervously, "to call him by his first name."

"The natives call him 'One-tusk,' but I didn't think that was a very dignified name for such a great animal. Apparently, he was speared as a youngster and the poachers got one tusk but something happened—he probably got up on his feet and scared hell out of them, so they didn't get the other. Look," Damien said, switching on his light again. "There he is!"

There he was indeed—a huge, magnificent elephant, calmly and daintily nibbling on some twigs and leaves from a giant tree. He blinked in the bright light, threw his trunk in the air in some sort of protest, then calmly went on eating.

Damien and Jenny drew closer; he held her hand and suddenly, she wasn't afraid any longer, not at all. She stood silently next to Damien, who had now let go her hand and had walked up to the beast, putting out one hand to quietly, kindly stroke the trunk.

"I'm surprised he remembers me," Damien said quietly. "I used to come here a lot, looking for him. Whenever I had something vital to decide, I'd look up old Max and talk to him. Maybe it was myself I was talking to, but he seemed to symbolize something to me. Max," he said, "go back to the herd and go to bed. If you hang around here all the time, they'll get the other tusk and the rest of you with it." He walked back to Jenny. "Come on—he'll probably be here all night—he isn't really hungry. I think he has trouble sleeping. But he'll be around for a long time; he's one of the smart ones."

When they were back in the truck, driving smoothly across the flatland, Jenny turned to look at Damien. His profile was clearly outlined in the moonlight.

"Thank you for bringing me," she said softly.

"My pleasure. We get around 2500 elephants here in the wet season. For a long time, they stayed away, probably because of the ivory hunters. Now, they're back, and of course, poachers are killing a lot of them."

"Damien?"

He glanced at her. "You aren't still frightened, are you?"

"Not a bit," Jenny said. "I want—I want to be able to feel the way you do in the jungle—at home, not afraid, at ease."

"Stay here long enough and you'll get that feeling," he told her. "Maybe you've got it now and you don't even know it."

"If I do," she said quietly, "it's because of you. Look, I don't want us to be unkind to each other. I don't want us to be . . . enemies."

"We never were."

"No," she said, "we never were."

The truck slowed down and stopped. Damien cut the lights and turned to her without saying a word. Jenny, as if spellbound, felt herself move closer to him on the seat, until their shoulders and arms touched.

"Will you tell me, Damien?"

"Tell you what?"

"Tell me about—about yourself. Please—I want to understand." She touched his hand, close by hers. "When I

124

brought the child to you today, I brought him because I knew you would help him, even though you don't seem interested in practicing medicine any longer."

He had started the truck once again. A certain coolness had come over him; the warm moment, the close feeling she'd experienced only seconds before was gone.

"That's right," he said, switching on the head lights. "I'm not interested."

"That's pretty difficult to understand."

"Then don't try. I'd better get you back; it's late."

They drove in silence until they reached the lodge. Then, in the parking lot, Jenny suddenly touched his hand once again.

"I'm sorry if I seemed to pry. I had no right."

He looked at her. Then she felt his hand on her face, warm and gentle, tracing the outline of her cheekbones, her temples; one finger lightly touched her mouth.

"People come to a place like this for a reason," he said. "It doesn't always turn out the way they thought it would."

"You think I've been foolish, don't you, Damien? Taking the children to Nairobi—if I hadn't done that, the child wouldn't have been hurt."

"He could have been hurt, or killed, some other way, Jenny. It just happened that he was with your group at the time. Look," he said quietly, "there's no harm in your taking the kids around to look at animals and there's no sense in your feeling guilty for any reason. In fact, I find that charming, your interest in children."

"I don't want you to find me charming!"

"Oh? And what do you want from me?"

"Nothing," she said loudly, reaching for the door handle, "nothing at all!"

She was outside, hurrying across the moonlit parking lot, up the porch steps, into the now-darkened lobby of the lodge. Two guests sat on the porch, drinks in hand; the women stared curiously as Jennifer fled into the lodge and down the long hall to the suite.

At the door, she fumbled for her key, suddenly realizing she had forgotten to bring it.

"It isn't locked," Damein said from behind her. He had followed her. "We never lock doors around here." He held the door open. "I'd like one more look at the boy before I turn in."

"Of course."

Jenny went into the softly scented room; the child was still comfortably asleep. While Damien bent over him, she sat on the nearby cot, taking off her sandals. Then, she waited silently, her heart beating in a mixture of emotions, as Damien quietly, gently covered the child once again.

"He'll be able to go home in the morning," he told her. "I'd suggest you take him by Dr. Du Mond's in a few days, just to be certain no infection has set in."

"I'll see to it," Jenny said.

He was looking at her. "Goodnight, then."

She started to speak, to say goodnight, to say something, but the words didn't come out. Instead, she stood by the cot; her feet were bare and under them, the floor felt smooth and cool and clean. Moonlight filled the room; the window she had opened earlier was still open, the scent of flowers, gardenias, came to them. From somewhere in the bush, a night bird called and another answered.

"Jenny." Damien came over to her, standing close, arms at his sides. "I want you to know that the jeeps will be there, at your aunt's, in the morning, for you to use."

"That won't be necessary," she said quickly. Her face was hot; she had the unexplainable urge to run out of there, to run from him and the wild feelings churning inside her. "Since you obviously think I'm simple-minded to want to change things—"

"I don't think that. I think you're very sweet and—"

"And a child. So much a child that I arm myself with

126

crayons and poster paper and think I can change an entire continent! Well for your information, Dr. Lear, I can't and I know it, but maybe, just maybe, the children can!"

"Where did you get the idea that I think of you as a child?"

"You—you just said—"

"I said nothing of the sort. As a matter of fact," he said, his voice low, husky, "I find you extremely appealing as a woman. You're very lovely, very—"

Their eyes met. Jenny's heart was thundering, a wild drumming in her ears; she moved like a sleepwalker into his arms and then, as he pulled her roughly to him, his mouth crushing down on hers, she yielded, gave herself to the moment, to this slot of time when the world was only silver moonlight and the heavy, musk-scent of jungle flowers and his arms and his body pressing down against hers with a fierce urgency and his mouth, moist and deep and full. . . .

Suddenly he left her, turned from her. He shook his head as if to clear it.

"Forgive me. I'll check on the boy before he leaves in the morning." He looked at her then, his eyes masked. "Goodnight."

She didn't answer. She was trembling, so much so that, when she heard him close the door softly behind him, she went to the window and sat on the floor by it, to let her burning face cool in the rain-washed night air.

What was wrong with her? How had it happened, this quick entrance into a world of symbols—the moonlight, the scents, the feelings she thought she had locked somewhere inside herself, perhaps forever, or at least until she could get her thinking straightened out completely. How had it happened, this sudden intrusion into her privacy by a man she hardly knew and wasn't even sure she liked?

And yet, back then, moments ago, her young body had arched toward his and her arms had wrapped themselves around him as his did her and she had, while he was kissing her, heard herself moan, as if she were already in a kind of dark ecstasy. . . .

All night, she tossed and turned on the little narrow cot. At dawn, the child woke up, spoke in a language she didn't understand, but she knew he wanted his breakfast and his mother, in that order.

She was in the bathroom taking a shower when Damien came back to check the child, who was not only up and feeling fine, but didn't want to leave without all his new presents. Through the closed door of the bathroom, Jenny could hear Damien's voice talking to the boy, teasing him, then, silence.

He was gone when she came out. She had dressed and now, she quickly combed her hair, sitting at the large dressing table in the room, carefully avoiding meeting her own feverish eyes in the glass.

One kiss, one brief moment of passion and need—and it was over. He had wanted her as much as she had wanted him, perhaps even more, but Damien had abruptly stepped back from her, avoiding her this morning, not even bothering to tell her goodbye.

So be it. She promised herself to avoid him at all costs. But the really troublesome thought was this: What if he was right, right about her plan, after all? What if she could never, ever change a single thing, what if she was only a silly, idealist female who had to have, as Damien had said, a "cause"?

Now that the rain had stopped, there seemed to be a new surge of energy at Maggie's place. A truckload of equipment arrived, and there was new fencing to be put up. That kept most of the men busy for a while, and because Jenny found she had trouble sleeping, she began to get up very early, long before dawn, going to the little desk near the porch to do the typing for her aunt. By seven, when Manguana served breakfast to the children, Jenny's chores were done for the day, except for helping to feed the animals.

Each day, Damien's truck and several jeeps arrived with their drivers. He may have thought her plan was foolish, but at least he kept his promise to furnish transportation to and from the city. For a week or so, she gathered up her little brood with their packed lunches and doggedly went in the truck to the city, where most of the day was spent in the library. Jennifer studied there, reading about ivory trading, trying to assimilate everything from why great swaths had been cut through forests along the Seronera River by elephants, to why big safari firms, places like Damien's lodge, were flourishing, making people very rich. Somewhere between poaching and hunting, there had to be another way, a better way for the animals.

Could she really change the children's thinking, so that as adults with families to care for, they would turn to some other way of making a living?

She returned to the reserve feeling very discouraged.

Maggie was on the porch, enjoying the view in a nicely mellow mood, possibly from the brandy she'd had with her after-dinner coffee.

"Jack and I used to take walks on nights like these," she said. "We'd never go far, never into the bush, just on the cleared meadow. On one of those very quiet, very beautiful nights, I decided I loved it here." She turned her head to look at quiet Jenny. "It came as a complete surprise; I thought I'd been dissatisfied and aching to go back home. It was a little like suddenly realizing you're in love with somebody you don't want to love."

"Aunt Maggie?"

"Yes, dear?" Her aunt put down her cup. "You aren't crying, are you?"

"I never cry, Aunt Maggie."

But she was; she was crying, and she was horribly ashamed of that fact. For nearly three days now, she had found herself waiting, waiting for something—she didn't know what—to happen. It was as if she were suspended in time, as if all her plans and her life here had come to some sort of standstill.

"Of course you are," Maggie said quietly. "You are crying, my dear, and that's a very good sign, you know."

Jennifer took a deep breath. For a moment, she didn't trust herself to speak; tears rolled silently down her face; her nose needed blowing and her throat felt full. It was true that she didn't cry, at least not very often and only for something that was deeply wounding her. She had cried at her mother's funeral, and years before that at her father's, but these present tears were embarrassing and baffling. She did not really know why she wept.

"Go ahead, dear," Maggie said gently. "It's good for a woman to let go once in a while, if only to make herself feel more of a woman."

"Aunt Maggie—that's silly!" Jenny wiped her eyes with a tissue her aunt handed her. "There," she said, "I'm finished with it. And I don't feel any more womanly than I did before I began."

"Well it ought to be good for something, Jenny." Maggie gazed out at the darkening jungle sky. "I think you'd better ask yourself what it is in your life that is making you unhappy."

"It's—I'm not sure." Jenny blew her nose, leaning back in her chair. She somehow felt better. Maybe it really was the good, cleansing cry, or perhaps it was that crying afforded her the opportunity to talk about things she'd been unable to bring up before. "I'll be sending that truck and those jeeps back to Damien in the morning," she said quietly. "It—it hasn't worked. I don't know why I thought it would, Aunt Maggie. I can't change anything here. I can't even take good care of the children."

"You mean the accident with the wire trap?"

"Yes," Jenny said. "That little boy might have died! He might have been hurt worse; Damien said he was very, very lucky."

"I see." Maggie was silent for a moment. "So you're giving up?"

"Yes; I'm afraid I am."

"There's more to it, Jennifer. What is it? Did something happen between you and Damien Lear?"

Jenny was very glad the light from the rushlamp was so dim; her face suddenly flamed.

"From the start, he hasn't put any stock in my great plans to reeducate the children about poaching, if that's what you mean."

"Well," Maggie said, "that isn't what I meant, but if you'd rather not talk about it—"

"There's nothing to talk about." The sudden memory of that deep and unexpectedly passionate kiss came to Jenny like a blow. She suddenly felt achingly lonely, almost bereft, as if she had lost something lovely.

Her aunt was watching her closely in the near-darkness.

"You musn't blame him, you know." Maggie reached out, gently patting Jennifer's hand. "Jenny, I told you before, it's not my place to speak of this; it isn't my place to tell you what happened to Damien Lear to make him feel the way he does about things."

"It doesn't matter," Jenny said, getting up from her chair. "I'll send his jeeps back in the morning and there won't be any more children caught in animal traps because of some silly idea of mine. Goodnight, Auntie."

"Jennifer, wait!" Maggie followed Jenny through the living room into the hallway. Here, the fiber rugs were cool under their feet and the smell of the jungle, musk mixed with flowers, was very pungent. Jenny felt dizzy, heady, ready to cry once again. "I don't ever want you to say it doesn't matter."

131

"Well it doesn't," Jenny told her. "Damien was right about my silly little outings—they were a futile waste of time and if it hadn't been for my—my do-goody ideas, that little boy wouldn't have gotten hurt!"

"Nonsense. The children around here play in the bush all the time. It's a part of their everyday lives. It wasn't because of you, my dear. You didn't put the traps there; the poachers did. You were trying to do away with them, just as I am. Now stop feeling sorry for yourself."

"Maggie, please, I'm very tired and I'm going to bed."

Her aunt's voice, quiet and yet firm, followed her up the stairs:

"Did Damien make love to you by any chance?"

Jenny froze on the stairs. She turned around, hoping her voice wouldn't tremble the way her insides seemed to be doing.

"I don't know how you can think—"

"I'm sorry," Maggie said gently. "It's none of my business, is it? But something happened; *he's* made you unhappy and you don't want to admit it!" She walked closer to the stairs, barely outlined in the shadows. "Jenny, he can't help it, you know. My husband used to tell me that Damien doesn't respond like other people because he can't, not anymore. Not after what happened to him."

Jenny's voice was very quiet. "What was it?"

"All right," Maggie said finally. "It was his child, his son. Damien brought his family here because he and Paul Du Mond planned to open up a clinic, a big free clinic. But Damien's wife hated it—she spent most of her time in London. She had an apartment there, they said, and the parties and men—never mind. It isn't for me to judge, and it wasn't that kind of thing that changed him."

Very quietly, Jenny came back down the stairs, facing Maggie.

"What did change him?"

Maggie looked at her. "His son died, of fever. That isn't

132

the medical term, of course, but a very high fever goes along with the illness. He'd been in Ghana with his mother and probably contracted it there. Anyway, Damien did everything he could, and so did Paul Du Mond, but the child died."

"I wish I had known," Jenny said, stunned. "I wish I'd known. . . ."

"His wife left Africa right after that and filed for divorce in London. I suppose Damien felt even more guilty after that; it was as if she was blaming him, you see, for having brought his family here. I understand he went into the bush and stayed with friends there, living in one of their huts, not practicing medicine and mostly drinking heavily. Anyway, when he came out, he built the lodge and began to get very rich indeed."

"Thank you," Jenny said unevenly, "for telling me."

"I still don't think he had any excuse at all for dropping out of life, however," Maggie said firmly. "Jack felt the same way, although he was a lot nicer about it than I am."

Jenny felt haunted all that night by her aunt's words. It was a long, lonely night, and she spent a great deal of it sitting by the window, looking out at the forest beyond, listening to the night sounds.

What Maggie had said was true, very true. Damien Lear had simply dropped out of life. He didn't care about anything.

Which meant, of course, that he could never really love a woman or be faithful to her.

EIGHT

Biano, the child who had been hurt, was waiting on the porch for Jennifer early the next morning. He limped slightly, but not much. In fact, he seemed very excited about what had happened to him and all the attention he'd been getting.

"We're going to be seeing Dr. Du Mond this morning," Jenny told him, lifting him into her aunt's Land-Rover. "Not the doctor who lives at the lodge."

She'd just rounded the curve, driving slowly, when the vehicles from Damien's passed her on the road. By the time she'd made a U-turn and headed back for Maggie's, the children who usually composed her little study group had all piled into the jeeps, ready, it seemed, for yet another day at the library, visiting curio shops or sitting quietly in the rain forest while she talked to them.

"Driver, will you please take those jeeps back to Dr. Lear's? Come on, children, we won't be going today."

Eyes misted, in some cases; there was a feeling of disappointment.

"You promised to talk about little moles today." The little boy's voice held a faint note of resentment.

"And you promised to tell us about the great marshal eagle!"

"I'm sorry," Jenny told them. "We just can't go until—until some other time." She felt their rising sadness. "Please, I'll bring you all a surprise, I promise!" She turned to the surprised drivers. "Thank Dr. Lear for me, please. Tell him I won't be needing them anymore." She would tell the children later that, although she would gladly take them on little visits to town, there would no longer be a class to teach.

She had started down the road, Biano next to her in the Rover, when she realized several children were running after her. She stopped and waited.

"We can't go with you? Everybody say we'll be good." He glared at Biano's bandaged leg. "Not go near the snares."

"I don't think it's a very good idea anymore," Jenny said gently. "I think you can have a better time helping my aunt. Or playing in the kitchen and talking to Manguana. She knows a whole lot more than I do."

"We like to draw the pictures."

Jenny smiled at him. "I know that, honey, but you don't need me for that. Now tell everybody not to chase after me when I start the car. I don't want anybody else getting hurt. Manguana is making honey cookies today, did you know that?"

But her heart felt very heavy as she drove off, leaving the little, sad-eyed band of children standing in the middle of the road. Damien's vehicles had already headed back toward the lodge; she had told the drivers not to come anymore with them.

So it was over, her great plan to change her part of the world.

She switched on the car radio. On one channel there was a newscast, and another station carried American western music; the rest was static. She tried to clear thoughts of Damien from her mind and get on to the next problem.

Which was, of course, whether or not to stay here in Africa. She was over her ex-boss now; she hadn't thought of him in ages, it seemed, except with a kind of vague disgust. Her aunt, whom she had supposed would be horribly lonely, actually wasn't; Maggie would be busy and involved until she died.

What was there here, then, to hold her?

* * *

135

The Du Monds' apartment was filled with waiting patients. Heller, wearing a white nurse's uniform, came out carrying a baby in her arms and smiled when she saw Jenny.

"I've been meaning to get over to your aunt's to thank you for the drawings you sent us," she said. "You'll see them inside, in Paul's office." Her eyes narrowed. "Are you okay? Don't tell me you're coming down with something, Jenny."

"I'm fine," Jenny told her, although she didn't really feel fine at all. Not sick, just strangely sad. The last time she had been here, she'd been with Damien. "I'm afraid Biano here got tangled up in a wire snare."

"I see he did." Heller bent over the child. "Hold still, darlin'." She straightened up. "It's clean as a whistle, but Paul will want to look at him anyway, I'm sure. Who took care of him?"

"Damien."

"It was an emergency measure, I imagine, right?"

"Yes. I took Biano to the lodge."

There was something, some look, in Heller's eyes. "And instead of having you come back there, he told you to bring him here to us?"

Jenny nodded. "Heller, I was wondering if I might speak to you later on."

"Sure. I'll try to get a minute between the next flu case and the lady with the broken toe. Just wait for me, okay?"

Jennifer waited patiently for nearly an hour. When everybody had been seen, when the last tearful child (he'd just been given a shot) was carried out by his mother, holding a honey bar in one small hand, both Paul and Heller came out to Jenny in the waiting room.

"We honestly meant to come by and say thanks for the kids' drawings," Paul told her, pulling on his pipe. "They're in my office; come and see."

They were indeed; they were tacked up all over. There was a bright crayon drawing of a slightly cross-eyed cheetah next to his medical degree from Paris.

"Dr. Du Mond—" Jennifer moved about the room, a glass of fruit juice in her hand. Heller had brought a tray with cookies for Biano.

"Call me Paul—I thought we'd all become friends."

"Paul—I've decided not to try to—to teach the children. I'm not even sure I want to stay here any longer." She put down her glass; her voice had taken on a husky quality. "Damien and I aren't—really friends, you know. I'm sure he's a very dear friend of yours, but I'm afraid I can't agree with his reasons for having given up."

Heller and Paul were watching her closely. Finally, Paul asked the question:

"Has someone told you about what happened to Damien?"

"Yes," Jenny said quietly. "My Aunt Maggie did. I think she wanted me to know so that I could draw more reasonable conclusions about him."

"I see." Paul went over to the window. "It's a city you hate sometimes," he said quietly. "Sometimes, I feel guilty as hell for having brought Heller here, staying here, making her live out her life with me in this bug-infested, disease-ridden—"

"All of which means," Heller interrupted cheerfully, "he's in love with the place. Where else can you look out your window and see flowers like we have here? Where else can you find the kind of mutualism the animals teach us? In the jungle, whatever happens—life, death—it's always for the best, always for the benefit of the creatures living there. I'm not talking about man's killing them, of course. I'm talking about the way God has allowed one creature to live because of another creature's existence. The next time you take the kids out for a walk, tell them about the swallows who feed above the buffalo, eating the insects the buffalo attracts."

"I told you," Jenny said, "I've decided not to—"

Someone had come into the outer room, the waiting room. Heller got up quickly, putting down her cup and opened the door to the office. Then, a wide smile came to her pretty face.

"Damien! What on earth are you doing in town?" She opened her arms and as Jenny watched, heart beginning to pound in something close to pleasure, Damien came into the room, hugged Heller and then, as his blue eyes caught sight of Jenny, an unmistakable look of gladness came into them.

"I'm here to borrow a few things," he said. "Forceps, for one thing, although I doubt if they'll be needed."

"Forceps!" Paul had turned from the window. "What's going on?"

"A friend of mine is making me keep a promise I made to him once," Damien said. "How are you, Jennifer? Well, I hope. And how's the patient today?" He leaned over the child on the floor. "Dr. Du Mond taking good care of you? I see you've got more honey bars than you can handle."

"Damien," Heller asked persistently, "would you mind telling us who is having a baby and why you're—"

"I promised the young chief I'd deliver his first-born, that's all. I stayed in his village for a while, a few years ago. This morning I got a message, so I'm on my way." He looked at Jennifer once again. "I was surprised to see all my drivers back at the lodge with the truck and jeeps."

"Yes," Jennifer said quietly. "I—I won't be needing them any longer. I planned to send a personal note to you, but I might as well thank you right now."

"You've given up on the kids then?"

Her face colored. Why did he always spoil the good moments by saying something or doing something to hurt her?

"Yes," she said coolly. "I've given up."

Heller quickly covered the bad moment by offering Damien tea, which he refused, saying he was in a hurry.

"I've probably got hours," he told them, "but anyway, these women are usually healthy and not at all afraid, so it probably won't take long. She's in first-stage labor now, according to the message."

"Good luck, old man," Paul told him. "Glad to see you're keeping your hand in. First the boy, now—"

"I'm still an innkeeper," Damien said. "I'm just keeping a promise, that's all. And yesterday, I frankly didn't have the courage to say no to Miss Logan. She's a very tough-minded girl." He smiled. "Why don't you come with me, Jenny?"

For a second, Jenny felt stunned with surprise. She'd felt sure he didn't want to see her again, that the kiss and embrace had only come from some physical need in him.

"I'm not sure I'd be any help," she said finally.

"Don't need help. The women there usually stand around and wail—it's part of the ceremony. There's bound to be a big feast afterwards, though, with dancing and singing. It's a time to remember." His eyes deepened. "I doubt if you'll find anything like it back in the States, in the discos."

"But I have to take Biano back."

"No, you don't," Heller said firmly. "I'll drive him back to your aunt's. I've been meaning to call on her anyway; one gets lonely for female talk sometimes. And God knows I wouldn't want to chat with those jet-set morons who stay at Damien's lodge! Go on, Jenny; you wouldn't want to miss this."

So Jenny found herself in Damien's truck once again, sitting next to him as he drove slowly through the crowded, teeming city, past the modern, whitewashed buildings to the European-influenced suburbs, and finally, past the squalid shacks that lined the road leading to the bush. Here, there were herds of cowlike wildebeests, tended by men in the traditional dress—sandals and a colorful, wrap-around robe. Damien honked as they drove past, and without fail, these native shepherds waved cheerfully.

"It's going to get dusty pretty soon," he told Jenny. "Better roll up the window."

In the closed-up cab of the truck, cooled by air-conditioning, she suddenly felt herself to be in a tight and intimate world with him. They were deeper into the jungle now; the road had narrowed and was pitted with holes.

"I'm sorry for what I said back there," he told her suddenly. "About your having given up, I mean. That wasn't a very civil way to put it."

"It was what you wanted me to do, wasn't it, Damien?"

He was silent for a moment. The greenness of the bush reflected itself against the glass windows; a horned eland stared at them silently as they passed by.

"I wanted you to understand that old ways die hard here, very hard. But I'm sorry for the kids—I know they'll miss being with you every day." He glanced at her. "I know I would."

Once again, she felt that sudden surge of something close to joy go through her. How odd that this man could do that to her; with a word, a glance, a smile, he could suddenly color her world.

"It was very kind of you to ask me to come with you," she said quietly. "I just hope I won't be in the way."

"You've got a special feeling for children, haven't you, Jennifer? Don't deny it; when you discover something you do very well, you shouldn't turn your back on it, you know. People who paint beautifully shouldn't decide to bake cookies for a living."

"I beg your pardon?"

"Now take Manguana," he said. "A very wise lady, very wise. She knows what she does best and she does it. Haven't you ever wondered where all those honey cakes come from that the Du Monds pass out to their patients? Manguana makes them. She has a lot to give to the kids." He began to slow the truck down as the road got steep and even more narrow. "Now you," he said, "you should be working with kids too. And painting, of course."

"How did you know I like to paint?"

"Your picture of the female monkey with her newborn was with the package of drawings that were sent to Heller and Paul. I hope you don't mind—I kept yours."

She had forgotten that she had sketched the monkey that day in the rain forest, while the children were coloring and drawing and having such a lovely time. So he had kept that!

"You'll find some beautiful views in the village," he told her. "Did Maggie ever take you here?"

"No."

"Have you ever heard the drums at night?"

Some sense of excitement touched her. "No, but I'd like to."

"This country," he said quietly, almost as if he were speaking to himself, "it grips you, holds you like a fist, and when you try to get away—you very often find you really don't want to."

"And you, Damien—do you want to?" She realized she wanted to touch him.

"Sometimes," he said softly.

They rode on into the nearby village in silence. Jenny's mind went back to her brief, sad conversation with Maggie; this man had suffered deeply and yet, he never spoke of it. How angry he must be, she thought, to have turned his back on medicine! How wounded, how deeply wounded his spirit must be, to call himself an innkeeper, to have decided he was no longer interested in saving human life, except to keep a promise or as a kind of polite accommodation, the way he had done for little Biano.

She found herself grasping for ways to talk about it, about his dead son, his little girl who was in school someplace—

London, Maggie had said. Some easy, polite way to say she was sorry, sorry his life had become ashes.

But he never allowed anyone to reach past his hurt; he was always, as far as she could tell, easygoing, flippant and caustic, treating life as if it were all some enormous joke, comic in its cruelty. And in some strange way she hadn't quite thought out yet, didn't fully understand, her knowing this about him, even understanding, in a way, that thick shawl of hardness he had drawn about himself as a kind of armor from further agony made her feel a different kind of love, different than the passionate rising of her feelings the time he had kissed her at his lodge. But it was love all the same, and its addition to the other only bound her closer to him, increasing her feelings for him.

This knowledge stunned her, made her sit beside him in a kind of muted resentment. She had not meant to fall in love. She had come here because something, some ugly thing in the guise of love had tricked her, nearly caused her to become a man's mistress. She had run from that, thank God, to a place where there were good women, Maggie and Manguana, living in a peaceful house in a land where New York's life style seemed very remote indeed. And shortly thereafter, she had been freed from her unhappy experience with Brendon so much so that it seemed, finally, as if a different person had once thought she loved him. . . .

And now this.

They went up another bumpy, rocky hill and then he stopped the truck and Jenny leaned forward to see. The windshield was somewhat scratched and quite dusty, so she opened the car door and got out, standing on the top of the hill. The view was spectacular; a warm, moist breeze blew up from the clean river beyond. It was sweet and fragrant, touching her hair and face.

"There it is," Damien said. The village lay in a thick clump of trees, nearly invisible from this vantage point. "We'd better leave the truck here," he told her. "Give me your hand. I keep telling Kuana that he ought to be ashamed of himself for not putting in a road, but he never does, the old fox. He doesn't want strangers bothering them. By the way, it's his daughter-in-law who's having the baby."

He helped her over a series of rocks; she was afraid, at first, because there was a steep drop, but then she very suddenly didn't feel afraid at all. It was beautiful to be here in this lush paradise with him, close to him, about to witness a miracle with him. She stumbled once; he caught her in his arms and then, he was looking down at her with some honest, surging need rising in his eyes. He bent his head, drew her body close to his, and then he kissed her mouth.

It was another moment of wild feelings, with the world gone for an instant; it was like being transported into some dark and secret and lovely place with him. It was like being a part of him entirely, totally belonging to him for an instant in time.

"I hope that little one isn't going to decide to be born in a hurry," he said then, smiling. "The young chief is one of my best buddies—he'd be very angry with me if I missed the big event."

She realized that he had once again assumed his light manner; as they pressed on, she began to realize that once again, Damien had put on his cloak of teasing toughness. *Isn't he ever going to say something to me that is real, that happened, that hurts him?*

Apparently not. They had reached a plateau in some way; she certainly wasn't going to mention his dead son, his divorce, any of it. If he only wanted them to be kissing friends, with a cheery, surface kind of relationship, then that was what she would accept.

The village lay in a kind of pocket, surrounded by heavy green trees and the most beautiful flowers Jennifer had ever seen. There were orchid trees everywhere, heavy with the gorgeous blossoms, violet hues and cream white and a very pure and beautiful pink. The people there lived in what were obviously permanent huts; there were hearty food gardens growing around them, and everything was very neat and clean-looking. Damien and Jenny had been met at the edge of the forest by the chief himself, a tall, very polite man who spoke no English.

She felt high on her present state of mind—being here with Damien, feeling a new closeness in her feelings for him. Once she had been able to accept the fact that, like it or not, she was in love with him, she had begun to enjoy it, *revel* in it.

She was happy, and strangely at peace, as she stood, during the birth of the child, in the back of the hut. Some very old women were given the place of honor around the grass mat on the floor where the young woman who was about to give birth squatted.

Damien leaned over the girl, talking softly to her. The watching women, including Jennifer, held hands; a young girl with strong, beautiful white teeth held Jenny's right hand while the mother-to-be's grandmother held the left. They made, in unison, a kind of singing, a soft and mellow sound like keening. It sounded like some kind of prayer, a lovely, soothing chant rather like the mourning sound of doves.

Jenny couldn't see much of what was going on, not until, when the chanting suddenly stopped, she gently pushed her way forward until she could see clearly. Damien had his hands on the girl's face. Her eyes were closed; she made no sound at all except, finally, a soft, low moan.

Then, holding Damien's hands, in a sitting-up position, she delivered her son.

The place was filled immediately with pure joy and goodness. One of the girls hugged Jenny, then another did, and she hugged back, crying and hugging everybody. She went closer to the baby; he was fat and beautiful.

It was night now; Jenny sat next to Damien on the hill facing the village. They had walked from the hut where the child had been born and even up here, they could hear the singing and joyful sounds coming from the village. There was a huge bonfire and the tantalizing aroma of well-spiced meat being cooked.

Jenny sat on a smooth rock. The light from torches cast a soft, orange-colored glow over the men and women who sang and danced in celebration.

"They liked you," he told her. "They're a very strong, independent people, you know. They were under British rule for a while, with all opposing parties done away with, that sort of thing. But not any longer. Frankly, I don't think they need anybody, not even a doctor."

"Something could have gone wrong," Jenny said practically.

"If it had," he told her, "they could probably have done as good a job as I could. Just because a man lives out here and doesn't read medical books, it doesn't mean he may not have his own methods of dealing with illness. Frankly, most qualified doctors are amazed at the cures that come from other means than cutting people open. We carve people up too much. Here, they depend on natural herbs and keep themselves and everything else very clean."

"Damien," she said carefully, choosing her words, "what you're really saying is that these people can get along just fine without a bona fide doctor. Somebody like you to look after them on a regular basis."

She realized, with a sinking feeling, that she had somehow spoiled the moment with her words as surely as if she had stood in front of a plate glass window and hurled a brick through it. Even in the moonlight, she could see the frost come into his blue eyes.

"If they need a bona fide doctor, as you call it, they can

find one. There are a lot of them in Nairobi, including Paul Du Mond."

"So you don't think it matters that you no longer practice? You don't think that's a terrible loss, a terrible waste of—"

"Kindly don't tell me I'm wasting my life. If I want to listen to that kind of garbage, I can go into any bar in Africa, sit down and tell them my life story and they'll tell me my life is wasted." He stood up impatiently. "Do me a favor and spare me the violins, will you?"

"I don't mean to pry," she said uneasily. "I know that— that when people are dreadfully unhappy, they sometimes don't think too clearly about what their priorities should be."

"Have you by any chance been talking to somebody? The Du Monds?"

Her hands suddenly felt moist. She did not want him angry with her; the coldness in his eyes wounded her. She hated that, that new sense of being so vulnerable, but for now she didn't try to fight it.

"I wanted to know about you," she said, her voice low. "I wasn't—I didn't mean to be nosy, it was only that I— was interested in you. I found myself wanting to know about you." She felt horribly humiliated having to explain. "I thought you might have told me, but when you didn't I suppose I just decided at some point to find out for myself. I'm sorry if that offends you in any way. I'm not trying to get into your private world, Doctor." She was not begging; some sense of pride or perhaps dignity had come to her, so that she found herself refusing to let his sudden withdrawal affect her.

"I have my reasons," he said, not looking at her. Then, he turned his head; she felt his steady, smoldering gaze on her. "Do you know what they are, Jenny?" His voice was quiet. "Did someone explain all of that to you, somebody who would like to make it all sound very twisted and not very gentlemanly, like somebody who decides to jump ship for some crazy reasons? Sorry," he said, "I don't feel that way."

"I know about your son, Damien."

The only thing that changed was his eyes. He shot her a quick, blazing look, brimming with sudden, spurting emotion, a look so filled with need that it was almost like a scream, a cry for help.

Then it was gone.

"Good. I'm the guy that people love to sit in taverns in Nairobi and get drunk reminiscing about. The local doctor who quit doctoring and decided to get rich instead, running a hotel nobody around here can afford to come to. I've accepted that," he said, and once again, that thread of amusement had crept in. "I'm very used to being the local antihero."

"How about becoming the local hero, instead?" Jenny said.

"How about minding your own damned business?" he said, his voice good-natured but his eyes cold.

And suddenly, as she started to saying something, something tinged with abruptness and anger, he grabbed her, pulled her roughly to him and closed his open mouth over hers. She struggled, tried to get away from him, but she seemed to grow suddenly tired, tired of not telling him she cared about him, that in spite of everything—including not wanting to—she did love him.

"You're very dear," he told her, his face in her long hair. He stood holding her; he had kissed her three times, deeply, and now they both were shaken, unwilling to let go of the sweet closeness. "I know," he said quietly. "I'm not doing what I ought to do, most of the time. I'm very aware of that. But I've made a conscious choice and I'm standing by it. If you and the rest of the world choose not to like that, it can't be helped."

She closed her eyes. "Please say it, Damien. Please,

please say you were very, very hurt when your son died and you couldn't go on with your life. That happens to people," she said gently. "It happens to people and then they get over things somehow and they go on with their lives."

"I'm doing that." He took his arms from her but before he did, there was a certain tightening of his fingers against her flesh, the beginning of anger, most likely. There were always signs, flashes that said quickly: *Don't interfere in my life!*

"No," Jenny said clearly. "No, you aren't. You came out here with Paul and Heller to help people and because you lost one of your own, you're going to give up, quit, hide out in that fancy lodge of yours. I'll bet you get drunk at least once a week so you can feel sorry for yourself!"

"It's time we left," he said grimly. There were wild orchids growing nearby; in a startling, sudden gesture of anger, he thrust them aside. The beautiful flowers lay in a crumpled heap.

"Damien—are you all right?"

"Of course. It's—my son used to have a little garden— he grew orchids there."

Without waiting for her to speak, he turned and strode down the hill, leaving her behind.

NINE

The celebration went on all night. Jennifer, having walked alone down the hill and back to the village, had sat among the women, the younger ones, and when they passed her a warm coconut shell filled with delicious, steaming food, she ate it, using her fingers, the way everybody else did. A few times she found herself looking for Damien, watching the hut of the chief, for it was surely there that Damien would be spending the night, while she herself had been assigned to sleep with some of the children.

But he was nowhere to be seen, and she finally concluded, with a sense of growing anger, that he had indeed gone to bed to sulk. *Let him then*, she told herself, with a surging new sense of conviction. *Let him sulk! I'm right; I'm absolutely right. He should be practicing medicine, not hiding himself in the bush, pretending to be an innkeeper, tricking himself into believing he can turn his back on life. . . .*

She sat cross-legged in front of the flickering fire, watching the people dance and talk, their voices soft over the Swahili vowels. *If I stay,* Jenny thought, dreamy now, dreamy and warmed as she sat with other girls by the fire, *If I stay, I'm going to learn to speak their language. That way, we can learn from each other—if I stay, I'm going to . . .*

And quite suddenly, she sat up straighter, putting down the now-empty coconut bowl, and she looked around the orange, flickering firelight at the faces, the black-satin faces, sleepy children and beautiful young girls and proud mothers and the old ones, gentled and loved by the whole tribe.

In that moment, Jennifer realized that she loved them, loved their children, and she could not, would not leave here. Not even Damien, who did not believe in anything she did, could force her to leave!

And so now she could sleep without worrying, without thinking about whether or not she would allow herself to be hurt by him. Only people in love could be wounded by the wrong word, the careless glance, the gesture that meant love was received but not given back. Or maybe not even available to give back. That might be it, after all; Damien might, at this point, be totally incapable of loving her or anybody else.

The child lying on the mat next to Jenny's crooned softly in her sleep and turned over, snuggling close to Jenny. Jenny's arms went around the little girl, and, feeling strangely strong and safe, Jenny slept in the sweet-earth smelling hut, with ten of the tribe's children.

There were shy goodbyes in the morning; Jenny gave away her mirror and her lipstick and a bottle of pink nail polish she found in the bottom of her purse. As a special gift to the new mother, she impulsively took off her watch and handed it to the chief. She pressed it into his hands, pointing to the hut where the new mother and baby were. The chief nodded and smiled at her.

"You handled yourself very well," Damien told her as his truck bounced them along, back to Maggie's. "Look—I'm sorry about last night. I was a bastard to bring you here and then ignore you part of the night." His words sounded heavy, as if it had been a struggle for him to apologize.

Jennifer said nothing. They rode along for a while and she was conscious of his taking sneak glances at her now and again.

"I said I'm sorry," he told her. "I'm usually a gentleman—ask Maggie if I'm not." His hand touched hers almost gingerly. "Jenny?"

"I'm still here."

"Will you forgive me? And let me take you to dinner tonight?"

She closed her eyes. It was a beautiful morning; green and still, with a silver-blue sky and no clouds. It was hard to realize that not far from here an animal might be lying bleeding and in agony, trapped by a snare of mesh wire and cruel snap clamps that might have caught his leg.

"I think it best we don't," she said quietly.

"I told you, I know I shouldn't have lost my temper the way I did. I—I'm very grateful to you for a lot of reasons and I want to go on seeing you. More importantly," he said, not looking at her, "I want you to want to go on seeing me."

"Why?"

"Why?" He shrugged. "Okay. If you really want to know, it's because I happen to like you very much. You—let's just say you're different."

"Different from whom?"

"There," Damien said, smiling now, "you see? Most women would be content to know they'd just had a very nice compliment laid on them. The lady has been told she is not only different from most women, but she is decidedly admired. Most females would just lie back and bask in that. You, however, don't. You keep pestering me. And," he said, "I hate that but I like it."

She turned her head quickly to look at him. Suddenly, it was all right, what he had done, the walking away from her; the dark, brooding anger and pain that had caused him to treat her that way had caught hold of him, that was all.

"Damien, I've decided to stay. And I've decided not to give up with the children." He turned to look at her, his blue eyes suddenly brimming with feeling, and at once, her heart lightened. "I'm not just going to take the little ones with me; I'm going after some of the older kids too, the ones in school. I can talk to their teachers and maybe get them to work along with me. For instance, did you know that the poachers' ringleaders ship skins from Kenya by way of forged export documents? Young people should know that. . . ."

She didn't realize it until they pulled up in front of Maggie's, but she had talked non-stop about her plans for her work with the children.

"Jenny," Damien said, looking totally charmed and amused at her eagerness, "Please change your mind about dinner."

"I don't see—"

"I'll give you the chance to tell me what I'm doing wrong all the time. I seem to make you very angry, did you realize that?"

She smiled. "Yes," she said softly, "you do make me angry."

"Good. Making up can be—"

"Damien," Jenny said firmly, getting out of the truck. "I have what I believe to be very serious business ahead of me. I'm going to spend most of my time trying to fight the killers who put up those snares." She took a deep breath. "Now a lot of those kids I'm talking about are going to begin to care—and I think that's important."

"I think it must be your face," he said slowly, eyes narrowing. "Yes; it's got to be your face. Or maybe it's something else—I don't know. All I know is that you can make me very very angry and I keep wanting to see you. Dinner, I promise you, will be private, delicious, and I'll behave myself. You, on the other hand, can tell me more about your project."

"Will you at least try to take me more seriously, Damien? I mean—my work."

"Only," he said lightly, "if you'll promise to take me less seriously. I'll be by about eight."

She found Maggie out in back in the round summerhouse, standing on a low ladder, stringing up strands of colored paper streamers.

"Hello," Maggie said, some of the paper held up between her teeth. "I was hoping you'd get back in time for the party. Hand me those flowers, dear."

"It looks lovely," Jenny said, handing her aunt the paper flowers. "What's the occasion?"

"I'm afraid I've forgotten. Jack used to keep a record of all the holidays here, so we'd know when to celebrate, but I never knew—I still don't. All I know is that Manguana asked me to give a party so I'm giving a party." She jumped down. "I know it's none of my business, dear, but did you by any chance spend the night with Damien Lear?"

"Yes—but I can—I mean, it wasn't—"

"I see. In other words, you fancy yourself to be in love with him."

"Aunt Maggie, I don't want to talk about it, I really don't."

"Very well then," Maggie said, beginning to gather up boxes of paper flowers. "But when you get hurt, don't say I didn't warn you." She headed for the kitchen. "I think today is in honor of the birthday of one of Massukuntna's ancestors. I hope I ordered enough Coca-Cola."

"Aunt Maggie," Jenny said worriedly, following her through the cool, freshly polished hallway into the living room, where Maggie, on her knees, began taking more decorations out of a big cardboard box. "What are you trying to tell me? Are you trying to tell me something to make me hate Damien? Is that it? Because if you are, that's totally unfair!" She had not meant to speak so bluntly, even rudely, and it surprised her a little to realize that she was so ready to defend her relationship with Damien.

"My only interest has been to keep you from getting hurt, Jennifer."

Jenny let her breath out. "I'm sorry. I guess maybe last night's events put a rosy glow on everything. I keep forgetting about the fact that there are a lot of things you say that I run from simply because they're true."

Maggie smiled. "Come and have some coffee. Did you know we had a baby elephant born last night? Looks just like Peanuts did. . . ."

It was a very nice day, a very happy day, one she would remember for a long, long time, trying to recapture in her mind the way she had felt this day, the day she had made up her mind to stay here and follow her dream. All of it, of course, had a great deal to do with Damien, although Jenny didn't really want to admit that to herself. She knew that she often saw his face; his image would come suddenly and abruptly and rudely into her mind as she was doing something else, thinking some practical thought or reminding herself of some chore she yet had to do, and there he would be, and she would remember his arms and his probing mouth on hers and she would suddenly feel changed, warmed, as if she had walked closer to the fire—

Or perhaps it was only a step to the edge of hell.

She walked with the smaller children to view the newborn elephant, who did indeed resemble Peanuts as she stood on wobbling, fat legs and nursed. Two of the children had witnessed the birth and they told Jenny about it in sweet, broken English, black eyes wide with wonder.

At teatime, Jenny took out a sky-blue dress, nearly the color of Damien's eyes, and she pressed it in the kitchen, heating the flat iron on Manguana's busy stove. There was semolina with brandy-soaked raisins baking in the oven; the large, clean kitchen was moist and warm and somehow very dear to Jenny as she stood by the open back windows ironing her blue dress. There were children huddled under the table, their favorite hiding place, looking at an animal book from the library, and upstairs, Maggie's voice could be heard talking to more children. *Family,* Jenny thought suddenly, looking at them, at the room, with its sun-bleached wooden table and the blackened pots and pans and in the darkening backyard, the crowned cranes with their beautiful golden halos. That's what they were, these gentle people, they were her family.

And that being so, what was Damien to her?

She took a shower when it was dark, standing under the smooth, flower-scented water for a long time. Then, with her hair wet, she hurried inside the house, her mind on the blue dress, getting her freshly washed hair dry enough so that she'd not look like she just came in out of a monsoon, and whether or not it would be wise to put on some of the perfume she'd brought from New York.

New York. She tried to think of it, only briefly, but she tried very hard and yet, only pictures, not feelings, came to her. She saw herself as if from a distance, a rather pretty young woman sitting in an empty office very late one night, standing at the long glass wall that looked out over the great city. Brendon's offices had been on the twenty-eighth floor of a skyscraper, and one wall of each room had been total glass. It had given one the scary feeling of standing somehow exposed to everything out there, although she had never stopped to consider just what she felt she ought to be hiding from.

There had been many nights when she would sit in the office, trying to find extra work to do, so that when he phoned her she would still be there. Just catching up on some odds and ends, she would say. The fact that she lied should have told her how wrong it all was, what a fearful mistake it was going to be. The truth was, she stayed there because she knew he usually went uptown to his club for a few drinks before heading back across town and then on to the suburbs where he lived. If he saw the light on in the office, he would probably stop downstairs and call up to find out what was going on. Later, she understood that he wanted her to be up there, so he could come up, so he could flatter her, appeal to her lonely, confused heart and get her to imagine herself to be in love with him.

It all seemed now as if it happened to someone else, some other poor, misguided girl. Why hadn't she known that love had nothing to do with the few times she allowed Brendon to kiss her there in the office?

City streets, cement, glass, stop lights, bars, and all the rest of it seemed very remote to her now, sitting in that warm, moist upper room, brushing her long damp hair, with the gardenias and orchids thick outside the screened windows, and the night birds beginning their calls in the nearby jungle.

She pulled her hair back, coiling it into a bun at the nape of her neck. Then, she opened the window, and with a kind of reverence, chose a very creamy and particularly beautiful gardenia, gently broke it from the vine, and tucked it into her hair at the back. In the light of the rush lamps, she looked flushed and, if she did say so herself, extremely pretty.

Maggie's grandfather clock downstairs in the front hall-way chimed a discreet eight-thirty. Well, it was like him to do that, to be late, perhaps to make certain she would not think he was running to her, or that he needed her.

At nine o'clock, however, she was beginning to ask herself just what her role, if any, should be. She was pretty sure she knew what he wanted her role to be, but that didn't mean she was going to be absolutely pliant, sitting around waiting for him to leave his wealthy friends at his inn or lodge or whatever it was and finally remember her.

He was now more than one hour late. Jenny sat on the porch, watching guests come to Maggie's party, families with children, the young missionary family and some shop-keepers from Nairobi and the nearest neighbor, a very old man who lived with his old daughter in a grass hut just outside the reserve.

"When Jack was courting me," Maggie said suddenly from behind her, "I used to have a rule: more than fifteen minutes but not less than thirty didn't mean a thing. Everybody in that big, crazy family of his drank, so I figured he'd stayed a bit longer at home to have another squiff with his dad. If he was more than thirty minutes late and he hadn't called, I knew something terrible had happened. Of course, he was never more than thirty minutes late, though, so I never had to put the rule to the test."

156

"Yes," Jenny admitted, "he's very late. I was just trying to decide whether or not to be angry, and I decided not to be. May I come to your party, Aunt Maggie?"

She was in the round summerhouse, with the decorations holding up beautifully, as Maggie said, when the message came. At first, for a wild, happy moment, Jenny thought it was surely Damien, two hours late, but finally here and in one piece. Then, as she walked quickly through the house, having run across the lawn to the back door, she saw the outline of the jeep parked in front of her aunt's house, and the driver getting out. It was one of the young black men who used to drive the children to the city and the library and back.

Maggie's words—*something terrible*—came into her mind and for a moment, Jenny felt only unreasonable fear rising hot in her, unthinkable that he would be hurt or dead—

"A message from Dr. Lear," the man said politely. He handed Jenny an envelope with the lodge's crest on one corner of it. Holding it in her trembling hand, she thanked the driver, shut the door, and then leaned against it, letting the panic ease out of her. *Foolish to have gotten so concerned about him when here I am, being stood up!*

The envelope was not sealed. The stationery was impersonal, the kind she felt certain he stocked every guest room with. The writing was in black ink, bold, blunt-looking script and the message straight to the point:

> *Unavoidable circumstances make it impossible tonight. Sorry. D. L.*

Disappointment, followed by a quick surging of pride, came over her. She put the message in the pocket of her skirt and walked back through the silent house to the back

157

door. Everybody out in the little summerhouse seemed to be having a wonderful time. They were chanting, all of them, and dancing around. The dance looked very African, but the minister and his wife were dancing as if they'd been born to it.

Beyond lay the mountains, giant shadows this time of night, and before them Africa spread herself out like a feast—the lush rain forest, the calm, infinitely blue lake, the flat places where wild animals ran in packs, so utterly free and beautiful, the flowers, so huge and fragrant they surely must have come from another world—

This *was* another world. And with or without Damien's love or support, she was going to stay, just as she'd decided the night before.

She was going to enjoy her life here. She would not run as she had done the last time, in New York. If Damien's treatment of her hurt, she could bear it, because now, she was far, far stronger than she had been before.

With a great sense of peace; she realized she was strong now, and she would stay.

The party had been over for more than an hour, and Jenny lay on her bed, eyes wide. She had enjoyed herself—danced, ate, and had two glasses of some kind of drink made from fermented rice, far too strong for her taste; she didn't like leaving reality. Her new-found reality was here, and she wanted to face it. She had thought she would sleep at once, when she got to bed, but she didn't.

Suddenly hungry, she sat up in bed, reaching for her flashlight. "I'd love a sandwich," she called to Maggie, who was sitting out on the porch. "Is there anything left?"

"We can heat up Manguana's couscous, if she left some wood for the stove."

And so they ate together, sitting on the porch, a comfortable silence between them. Maggie had made spiced tea, and when the dawn began to show its coming, the black night sky began to be streaked with strands of silver, and then came the first pink blush over the horizon. Maggie stood up to watch it all happen and so did Jenny.

"Aunt Maggie?"

"Yes, dear?"

"I'm staying. I mean—for good. Even though things aren't—even though Damien and I are at odds when I'd rather we weren't—I'm still staying."

"Yes," Maggie said quietly, "I thought you'd get around to that. For a while, I must admit I thought you were just trying to dream up some impossible chore so that you could trick yourself into believing you weren't hanging around because of Damien Lear. But then that changed, Jenny. Now, I'm sure you're very sincere, and of course, that's the first step in a long series of steps that Jack and I took and that I'm still taking."

"Steps?"

Maggie nodded, beginning to gather up the plates and silverware. The sky had turned a bright pink in places; it was filled up with color. "You'll find that sincerity means you're under some kind of spell. That you think this place, with all its faults, is actually a kind of Eden. A savage Eden, but paradise, none the less. Well it isn't, my dear, and once you're able to accept the fact that it isn't, then you can remain here with a calm heart and no illusions."

There was no use trying to go back to bed now, Jenny decided. Instead, having said goodnight once again to Maggie, she dressed in jeans and a loosely fitting shirt, took her paints and equipment and set up shop on the rear porch. As she worked, she began to feel tension leaving her; it was lovely, catching, or nearly so, the exact blue of the lake, the rose color of the morning sky. As she painted, two giraffes browsed along, turning gold-pink in the reflected light, and Jenny very quickly sketched them into the background.

Manguana came, nodding and taking off her sandals to

pad barefoot through the house to the kitchen. Almost at once, delicious smells began to filter through the house, coffee and the sweetish aroma of frying eggs and sometime later, bread baking.

Tired now, Jenny leaned back and looked hard at her work. It had been a long time since she'd wanted to paint as badly as she had a few hours earlier, and from this one fact alone came a kind of strength, a feeling that her day could be a good day, with or without Damien in it.

"Very nice, Jenny dear." Maggie yawned, wearing her robe. "Those bloody jeeps woke me up."

"Jeeps! You mean he—did Damien send them again?"

"I'm afraid so. I'm surprised you didn't hear them. I guess one of the children must have been banging on the piano. At any rate, you'll find them lined up in front, as usual."

"May I use your Rover today, Auntie?"

"Of course. You can pile a heap of kids in that thing."

So she didn't need him, didn't need his jeeps, and she would tell him so herself!

Maggie was right; there was enough room for the usual number of children to go, although they were a bit packed in. But they were a cheerful, merry little bunch, armed with their crayons and their poster paper and their library books. Jenny gave orders to the drivers to head back to the lodge, and she followed them, bumping along over the uneven road until at last, they drove in a single line up to the front of the lodge.

It was nearly ten now; the morning had begun in earnest. White-coated waiters served continental breakfasts to guests; at one end of the awninged porch a group with a guide prepared to leave on safari. Jenny, ignoring the curious stares, walked quickly up the porch steps, calmly into the main room and then, straight across the polished floor to Damien's office.

"Please," a voice, very worried, said from behind. "The doctor is not in, Madame. He is having his breakfast."

"I see. And where is that?"

"On the east porch, the upstairs veranda, Madame. At the moment, he is—"

"Excuse me," Jenny said politely, walking past him. "You needn't announce me."

She hadn't the faintest idea where the east porch's upstairs veranda was but it certainly had to be upstairs. She had been followed halfway up by the pleading but polite man from behind the front desk, but he apparently had given up and left her to wander about upstairs. These were guest rooms, fronted by a wide hallway with a soft green carpet. The motif was pure African, all done by some clever designer to make the indoors seem like outdoors. Some of the bedroom doors were open, showing sunny rooms, beautifully furnished in subtle and exotic colors. A small hallway to her left showed some kind of porch. She went through and found herself on a wide, shady upstairs veranda, with lush hanging plants everywhere. Now, to find the east porch—

She heard his voice then; slightly loud, and the clatter of silver or a spoon against a cup. Jenny walked forward, coming to a little bend in the structure. Then the porch widened, and at the end, a small table had been set up, covered with a floor-length cloth.

Damien sat facing Jenny; a look of surprise and then something else came to his face. He looked vastly uncomfortable.

The woman's back was to Jenny. She was a silvery blonde and her slender, pretty arms looked white, not tanned, so she must have just recently arrived. She turned partially in her chair and stared rudely at Jenny, who, at that moment, seemed to have trouble finding her voice.

"I—returned your jeeps, Dr. Lear."

"No need to." He had stood up; his face was slowly turning a burning, embarrassed red.

"I won't be needing them."

161

And of course, he was about to begin tedious introductions; Jenny spared them all that by turning on her heel and walking quickly around the corner of the veranda, and then, when they couldn't see her, running the length of it to the door that would take her down yet another flight of stairs, down the hallway and into the lobby and at last, down the porch steps, into Maggie's waiting Rover and away from there, away from him.

In the cool library, she finally managed to calm down, control her thoughts, and get to the business of researching the mating habits of the sable antelope. Then she took the children to lunch, but not at the usual café. They had spiced fish spread on thick white bread and cold bottles of canned fruit drink; they were all in very high spirits.

In the park, Jenny told them about elephants along the Seronera River, and invited them to bring their friends to view the new baby elephant at the reserve. She decided to have a baby elephant-naming contest; surely if they loved this new creature they would, at some later point in their lives, find it very difficult to shoot or spear or set a trap for a wild elephant in order to sell his tusks and teeth for money!

It was suppertime when she pulled up in front of Maggie's with her sleepy little band. The children tumbled out; Manguana was waiting on the porch with a pitcher brimming with cold milk and a tray of goat-cheese sandwiches.

"Nothing for me, thank you, Manguana. I'm going straight to bed."

"First drink the goat's milk," Manguana said wisely. "It's rich and sweet—makes you feel nice and sassy."

Jenny smiled. "I'm afraid I'm in no mood to be—" She heard a sound; a door opened from somewhere downstairs. Was that pipe smoke she smelled? "Is someone here, Manguana?"

"In the library, Missy."

The library was a large, airy room where Maggie kept

all her late husband's manuscripts and books. Now, the door was partially opened. Jennifer walked toward it as Maggie swept out, looking slightly flushed.

"Good evening, Jennifer," she said somewhat stiffly and headed directly for the stairs.

"Aunt Maggie—what—" Jenny had reached the room and now, she opened the door and looked in.

Damien sat in one of Maggie's chairs, looking as if he might go into a rage any second.

TEN

There was a brief moment of mutual anger—*How dare he come here and behave as if he's some kind of warlord!* Jennifer started to turn and leave, before they began to argue. Somewhere behind her eyes there were tears; she had a horrible mental picture of herself sitting on the bottom step of the stairs, weeping like a child.

"Just a moment," he said, and in two giant steps or so, he had a tight hold of her arm. "I want to talk to you."

"Of course," Jenny said softly, sweetly, "but not now. I'm very busy—"

"Listen, dammit—I wanted to explain—"

She pulled her arm from his grasp. Her heart was pounding now and she realized she had somehow gone beyond the tears to a kind of calm, cool, and collected anger. Invisible anger, the best kind, because he would not see it, would not know how he managed always to churn up her feelings.

"When are you going to understand, Dr. Lear, that there is absolutely no reason for you to feel you must make some—some statement to me about your comings and goings? You've no need to defend yourself because as I be-

163

lieve I told you, I'm very busy with my work here. I have a job to do here that I believe in, and in spite of the fact that you think it's a joke, it just might turn out to be something very important!"

She had started for the staircase, not to cry on it but to return to her room and get to work on letters to the nearby schools.

"Jennifer, will you listen to me?" He followed her to the stairs, looking up at her as she began the ascent. "Jenny, I came here to talk to you about my daughter!"

She slowed, stopped, turned around and looked down at him.

"I beg your pardon?"

"Judy, my little girl. I want you to include her in your field trips from now until she leaves. Will you?"

She felt stunned, unable to grasp what he was saying to her.

"Your daughter is here, in Africa?"

His eyes were steady. "She arrived last night, with her mother. You didn't give me a chance to explain to you, and you certainly didn't give me a chance to introduce you to my ex-wife, Judy Anne's mother."

Jenny felt her face color. "I'm sorry. Perhaps if you'd been more revealing in your note, I'd have been more understanding. Good evening, Doctor. I'll see to it that— Judy, is it?—will be picked up in the morning. Kindly have her ready and waiting on the porch; I'll provide her lunch. We usually return—"

"I know what time you usually return. Will you have dinner with me tonight? No more surprises, I promise. Her mother vowed she had to talk to me about Judy and that was why the cozy little meal. Please, try to understand."

"I do," Jenny said quietly, "I do understand. I understand that your family is here from London or someplace and if you think that for a moment, I'd ever interfere with—with a man and his wife—" She looked at him. "I

164

did that once. I wasn't—we didn't—but all the same, I took something from his marriage simply by wanting to be with him, be near him, look at him. That was wrong, Damien, and I'm not ever, ever going to put myself in that position again!"

She was in her room, door closed, when she heard the sound of his truck starting.

And of course, she thought about that woman, his ex-wife, who had sat on the veranda across what appeared to be a very lovely table; she had sat across from Damien and when she had finally turned to look at her, Jenny had seen a beautiful face, delicately fragile, with a fine straight nose and expertly made-up eyes and a pretty, pouting little mouth. It was the face of a lovely woman who was quite used to getting her way with men.

After all, he had stood her up, hadn't he? And written a very terse, even rude note, simply saying he couldn't help it but he wasn't interested in seeing her. He certainly hadn't been very interested in seeing her when she had quite suddenly appeared on the upstairs porch!

She wondered if by some outside chance, he wanted to keep his ex-wife's attention, perhaps make love to her while she was here—and have handy little Jennifer waiting in the wings, so that when his beautiful Pamela went back to London, he'd have—

That, Jenny told herself firmly, *is quite enough of that line of thinking, thank you! Whatever is happening right now, or did happen, has nothing at all to do with your life! Kindly remember that and do not, repeat, do not make a fool of yourself by being jealous!*

She wrote the letters to the schools, got correct addresses from Maggie, and put them on her nighttable, so as not to forget to take them to Nairobi tomorrow, when she once again went in with the children. She envisioned seminars in mud-walled village schools, around campfires, and in some kind of club buses, touring with the children, going to different national game parks. The kids could become as knowledgeable and as dedicated as the experts, like Maggie.

There was definitely no time to let herself cry over Damien Lear.

She was up early the next morning but not before Maggie.

"Well," Maggie said, looking up from her morning tea. "I hear his little girl came along too." She put down her cup. "In case you're wondering how I found out, I told you before, news travels very fast here, very fast indeed. Manguana has a cousin who is employed at the lodge, you see, so almost as soon as they knew that our doctor friend was to pick up his ex-wife and daughter at the airport, we knew about it too. I would have told you, dear, but as I recall, you simply wouldn't give me a chance."

"It's nothing to me," Jenny said, reaching for the juice. "He asked me to pick up his daughter and take her along with the rest of the group while she's here." She looked at her aunt. Suddenly, she softened. "I saw his wife yesterday, Aunt Maggie. I didn't mean to spy, but for some reason, when he stood me up the way he did, I guess I just wanted to—to spit in his eye or something. That was what I was really doing when I decided to tell him not to send 'round his jeeps any longer. And there he was, sitting with—with Pamela and she was—"

"Beautiful?" Maggie's voice was calm. "Oh yes; she is that, all right. She was always very social, too; Jack and I would run into them sometimes at social things on the Ivory Coast. She always dressed expensively and with great taste, while he, poor man, always looked as if he'd far rather be doing something with his sleeves rolled up. They were, to say the least, an unlikely-looking couple." She leaned closer to Jennifer. "Are you ready to hear more about that so-called lady, Jenny? Because this one time, I am going to forget that I detest gossip, and I am going to

166

tell you some things about Pamela Lear that will make your hair stand on end! She hated Africa, tried every way she knew to make him give up the idea of starting that clinic, discouraged him at every turn. She made him feel foolish and idealistic and I wouldn't be at all surprised if she didn't cause him to lose his manhood for a while. I daresay that would explain all the women he's been with since—"

"Aunt Maggie," Jenny said, starting to leave the table, "I don't want to hear or know anything about the two of them!"

The two of them.

Try as she would not to think about what that meant, she did think about it; in fact, as she showered and dressed for the long day, she finally allowed herself to give in to that train of thought, to examine it and then put it away forever.

Damien had been married to a beautiful, if unfaithful woman, and now she had come back to him, which wasn't any of Jenny's business, and she vowed not to let Maggie say anything more; she'd heard quite enough. The fact was, at this very moment, that cool-eyed, silver-blond woman who had borne children by Damien might be in his arms, in his bed. And she, Jennifer, must face that fact.

She told the children about Judy before they left Maggie's, the usual, well-scrubbed little group, carrying their lunches in sacks. There was an extra lunch for Damien's daughter, and the children who spoke English were told to be very kind to the new little girl.

Jenny had absolutely no preconceived notions about the child, so that when the Rover pulled up in front of Damien's lodge and for the first time Jenny saw her, she was not ready for the delicately lovely little girl who primly and somehow shyly came along down the porch steps and introduced herself to Jenny and the others while her father watched from the doorway. She had a lovely, crisp little accent, picked up at school in London no doubt, and Jenny immediately began to love her.

All day, she found herself watching Judy without letting the child know. The little girl, although always polite and cordial, seemed not really to join in. In the rain forest, where they went to have lunch, they ended their day by holding hands and singing songs in English; the children who didn't understand all the words nonetheless understood that it was about a great lion who was smarter than the men who hunted him. After a few verses, repeated over and over, little Judy knew the simple words, but there seemed to be no joy in her singing, and once, she looked across the circle of children and Jenny saw in those eyes, the same blue as Damien's, his own reflected agony.

The child is desperately unhappy, Jenny thought clearly, and it was as if a knife had gone into her heart. She did not know if Judy Anne meant so much to her because she was Damien's child or only because she was an unhappy child.

She drove straight to the lodge after that; some of the children had nodded off, the way they always did at the end of the day, but sitting there beside her, Judy was wide awake.

"I hope you're going to be staying with us a while," Jenny told her. "We do a lot of interesting things, you know. Perhaps you'd like to do a drawing for us and bring it tomorrow, Judy. Do you remember the herd of wildebeests we saw back there? Could you draw them, do you think?"

"I'll try," Judy Anne said. She was seven, a slender little thing with pale blond hair and those startlingly blue eyes that Damien had. Beauty had stamped itself on her lovely face; she would be breathtakingly beautiful as a woman. "But I may not be staying very long, you see. Mother told me we might be going back to London soon."

"I see. I'd hoped you would stay longer and make more friends."

"I thought I'd be staying," Judy said, turning her head to gaze at Jennifer. "But it's my father, you see. Are you a friend of my father's?"

"Why," Jenny said, flustered, "I—I guess so. Yes; of course. He's a very nice man."

"He isn't at all nice."

Jenny took a small breath. "I'm sure," she said carefully, "that your father loves you very much, Judy. Look, tomorrow we'll all sit quietly on the library lawn and the other children will talk about stores—shops—that sell animal skins. The next day, we'll go and visit some. You aren't afraid of little snakes, are you? Because the next day, we're going to study them and maybe even touch one."

"I'll have to ask my father if he'll let me stay on a little while," Judy said, primly folding her tiny hands in her lap. "He doesn't want to, you see."

"I'm sure he does, honey."

"Oh no," the child said, and she seemed oddly adult, as if this was a simple fact of life. "He doesn't want me at all. My mother brought me here because she can't take care of me and she wants my father to do it. But he doesn't want to."

Either. The word came to Jenny's mind and stayed there. Ugly, terrible to think two people, parents, would not want this lovely child. . . .

Pamela and Damien stood on the porch of his lodge with a small group of guests. They all held cocktail glasses, and when Jenny pulled up in the Rover, hot, dusty, tired and angry, she got out, held Judy's hand and walked with her up the lodge steps. Pamela watched, gray eyes narrowing as Jenny walked toward her.

"Hello, darling," Pamela said to Judy. "Did you have a fun time?"

"I'm going to draw a lion, Mother. For tomorrow. I can go tomorrow, can't I?"

Pamela, looking directly at Jenny, smiled coldly.

"We'll have to ask your baby-sitter, darling. Would you mind awfully if my daughter tags along? I'm afraid she's a dreadful crybaby—did she do that today, Miss Logan?"

"Of course not," Jenny told her. "She was lovely, a perfect lady. Please allow her to come tomorrow; we love having her and," she said carefully, "I'm not a baby-sitter."

Pamela turned to speak to Damien, who had come over to them, carrying his drink. Jenny carefully avoided meeting his eyes.

"I was just saying that Judy's father is very lucky to have a young American girl living so close by," Pamela said sweetly. "So—convenient."

"Pamela has a remarkable ability to insult people," Damien said lazily. "I see you haven't lost the knack for it, my pet. Drink, Jennifer?"

"No, thank you. I have to get the other children home."

"Why not give them supper here, then I'll see to it that my drivers go with you. I'll send one of them ahead, to tell your aunt and the kids' parents."

"I don't—"

"Please," Damien said, his voice low, "my daughter has been very lonely. Having the kids here would be good for her."

Before Jennifer had a chance to answer, Pamela cut in. "It's amusing, darling, the way you want her to be happy on one hand and on the other, you can't be bothered with her." She raised her glass. "Here's to the Father of the Year, everybody!"

It was a monstrous moment; Damien turning on his heel and walking quickly inside, slamming the wide front door behind him. Other guests on the porch looked vastly ill-at-ease, and little Judy stood there about to cry.

"Of course we'll stay," Jenny said quickly. She gently touched Judy's soft hair. "Go and tell your father I said thank you very much indeed." She looked into Pamela's frosty gray eyes. "You're very blessed, Mrs. Lear, to have such a wonderful child."

"Tell that to her father, will you?" Pamela walked away; someone came up and poured more champagne in her empty glass.

Yes, Jenny thought suddenly, *I will tell him!*

She walked across the porch, but inside the lobby someone came up to her and, handing her a glass of wine, began talking about New York. It was a man, a tanned, handsome, probably rich young man here, he said, on safari. He spent most of his time working for his father in New York; he'd heard there was a beautiful American girl from the East living nearby and he was delighted she'd stopped by.

Jenny took a small sip of the wine and told herself to relax, to wait until the proper time. The evening stretched out ahead of them; there would be the right time to ask Damien why he was rejecting his child, when she obviously needed someone to love her.

Tables were set up on the porch; the staff obviously was surprised that children were allowed at the lodge; they ran around having a marvelous time, delighting and charming all the guests. There didn't seem to be one grump in the place, Jenny noticed; they all seemed to enjoy watching the kids.

Candles were lit at dusk and the children, including little Judy, sat at little tables fashioned from packing crates in the storage room, then covered with very elegant cloths. Jenny, declining the handwritten request brought to her by one of the white-coated staff members asking her to join Dr. Lear and the others in his private dining room, sat on the porch instead to watch the children enjoy themselves. From time to time, one of them would bring her something delicious they wanted her to eat, taken from their plates. It was one of the ways they told her they loved her so she ate every piece of bread, every little bite of potato or vegetable or meat that they brought her.

Finally she was quite full. She sat in one of the chairs, with Judy sitting next to her. It was a peaceful moment; the children were happy and well-fed and they'd all had a very good time, including Judy.

"There you are," Pamela said from the doorway. She walked across the porch rather unsteadily; she still carried the glass of champagne in her hand. Her pretty face looked flushed and cross in the moonlight. "Time for bed, Judith, and no whining, please."

"But the other children are still—"

"Mother doesn't give a damn about the other children, darling. Now go upstairs and go to bed." She shot Jenny a quick look. "Damien missed you at dinner, or did you know that? I really think he'd much prefer to sit out here with you, instead of inside with the rest of us."

"That's very flattering," Jenny said uncomfortably, "but I'm sure it isn't so. If you'll excuse me, Mrs. Lear, I think I'd better be getting the children back. Goodnight. Goodnight, Judy."

She left quickly, getting the kids into Maggie's Land-Rover. Then she reluctantly walked back up the porch steps, into the lobby and, into the bar, looking for Damien.

He sat at the end, surrounded by several women who alternately leaned on him, leaned against him, and leaned low enough to make their breasts quite obvious.

"Disgusting," Pamela said from behind, her voice thick and amused. "Little do they know that Damien is absolutely turned off by such vulgar displays." She smiled coldly at Jennifer. "You're in love with him, aren't you? Oh—don't deny it; I saw it in your eyes. How much, may I ask, do you know about me?"

"All I care to," Jenny said crisply, and she walked right on by, across the room, to stand squarely in front of Damien.

"I'd like to speak to you," she said quietly. "Alone."

ELEVEN

Damien gently shouldered his way from the bar to his office with Jenny following close behind him. Most of the men smiled her way; a few of them tried to convince her to join their party.

He closed the door of his office behind them and headed straight for the small portable bar near the long window.

"Drink, Miss Logan? Or would you consider that a step into debauchery?"

"Damien," she said clearly, "I want to talk to you about your daughter."

He was not looking at her and she had the feeling that when and if he did, his eyes would be masked, their secret hidden somewhere in the blue depths.

"Charming kid, isn't she? As beautiful as her mother."

"What kind of beauty are you talking about? The kind that hurts children?" Jenny stood her ground. "All right, look startled. I mean what I say."

"Well, the little cricket-by-the-fire turns out to be a tiger in disguise! It isn't nice," he said, putting ice into his rather stout-looking glass of whisky, "to talk badly about the mother of one's child. So I never do it."

"I know it's obviously none of my business," Jenny said evenly, "but she—your daughter—told me that you don't want her. She actually thinks you don't want her! And frankly, she looks so—so unhappy, for a little child—"

"She's quite right," Damien said at once. "I don't want her." He tilted the glass to his mouth, avoiding Jenny's stunned look. "At least, I don't want her here, here in the bush. I told you before, little Jenny, this place is not what it appears to be. It is filled with death traps. And it is no place for a child."

"Damien, she seemed happy with us today, at least part of the time. For an instant or so, there would be flashes of gladness in her little face; I honestly think she could get better here."

"My daughter isn't ill, thank you. I'm a physician; I ought to know."

"Are you, Damien? I thought you'd quit that. I thought the closest you ever got to practicing medicine anymore was to watch a woman have a baby as a favor to her husband and father-in-law, or looking after a child with a hurt leg only because you had to—"

"Is that why you wanted to see me, to tell me this?" He put down his glass, then began refilling it.

"Look," she said, "I know we don't agree on very many things. But what I'm doing is good for the kids, Damien, and it was good for your daughter! Why won't you let her be a part of it? You've a beautiful place here to make a home for her, and there are all these children to be her friends, and when she's ready to go back to school, there are very good ones in Nairobi, I understand—"

Suddenly, he slammed his glass down with a loud thud. His eyes were blazing with emotion. "I know about the schools, Jennifer! I had a son, remember? I had a boy who died in this cursed place, of an illness I couldn't stop; nobody could stop it. I'm not taking any chances on losing my daughter too, do you understand that?" He turned to the window; his wide shoulders seemed to fill the space of glass. "Judith Ann is returning with her mother to London. And that's final."

The seconds ticked by; the silence was hostile. Jennifer turned to leave, but suddenly, he bolted across the room, caught her with one hand and before she could move, he pulled her to him; one of her hands shot out to push him away but it was too late; he was kissing her. There was anger in that kiss, and as his kiss grew deeper and wilder, Jennifer felt both excited and insulted. She felt herself sinking, giving in; she felt the deep yearning, the attraction to him begin to overtake all reason, but then, in her mind's eye, she saw his child, his little girl, lonely eyes wide in that lovely face. . . .

She raised her hand—she had pulled away from him at last—and soundly, with full thrust ahead, she slapped his face.

They stood facing each other. He had gone quite pale.

"Your daughter needs you," Jenny said quietly. "I don't."

She opened the door and walked out into the hallway. Just beyond, the guests seemed to be having a wonderful, noisy time. Jenny pressed her way through, hurried down the porch steps, and got into the waiting Rover with the children.

It had been a nasty scene, a brutal confrontation, and it left her shaken. At Maggie's, she went quickly to her room, washing her face in the fresh, cool water in the basin. Her mouth felt bruised, violated; she hated him for having kissed her that way against her will, as if to physically overpower her would prove something to them both.

Maggie was outside feeding the animals when Jenny left the next morning. She piled the children in the Rover and headed down the bumpy road toward the lodge. It would be painful to see Damien this morning; she actually hoped she wouldn't because she wasn't at all sure about her feelings. She did not understand how she could feel anything but anger concerning him, and yet, close to him, she always seemed to black out, to forget everything except that closeness.

The jeep rounded the corner, nearly forcing them off the road. Jenny stopped the Rover, opened the door on her side, and leaned out.

"Is that you, Biwauka?"

He grinned. "Yes, Missy. Dr. Lear says you don't need to come by because his daughter isn't there."

"You mean she's gone off to London with her mother?"

He nodded. "Early this morning, to get early plane out. So the doctor sent me along to tell you."

"I see." Jenny experienced a feeling of sadness. "Thank you."

It was a long but fruitful day. Between lunch and tea, she and the children researched Serengeti lions and they talked about how, outside the parks and reserves, the lion might soon be gone forever.

But Jenny's mind kept wandering; she kept seeing that sad but eager little face, Judy looking at a picture book, singing with the others, holding Jenny's hand. *I could easily have loved her as my own*, she thought at one point, and she wished fervently she had never met Damien Lear.

They got back to Maggie's shortly before dusk. The children scurried all over the place as they always did; Jenny had stopped to glance at the hallway table to see if there was mail for her. Maggie had promised to try to get her on the payroll as extra help; if that didn't work out, Jenny knew she could probably get something for her paintings, enough to pay her room and board here and maybe buy an old bus to transport the kids back and forth in—

She was still standing there when she heard the truck roar up out in front.

She half-turned, then, seeing Damien striding quickly up the front steps, she picked up the letter postmarked New York and fled for the stairs.

"Jennifer!" His voice was like thunder.

She stopped at the bottom of the stairs, hoping, praying she would not have to face him.

"What the devil have you done with my daughter?"

She turned quickly around. "Judy? Why—I haven't done—I didn't pick her up today, if that's what you mean."

"Are you saying you haven't seen her all day, she hasn't been with you?"

She saw his eyes; they held a totally new look, a burning look filled with fear and anguish.

"Your driver brought a message," Jenny said, suddenly wanting to put her arms around him. "He told me you'd said not to stop by because Judy and her mother had left early. Damien, what is it?"

"She's gone," he said heavily. "I've got an emergency call in to Pamela, at Heathrow in London, but God knows when she'll show up in England—she'll probably stop in Paris to go to a fool party or something—" He shook his head, turning away from her to stare out the open front door. "Judy's out there somewhere. As far as we can tell, she ran away sometime last night."

"Ran away? Oh Damien—" Jenny went up to him, touching his arm. But she couldn't help but look out there too, to where the lawn ended and the deep underbrush began. Out there, not too far away, hidden from the casual eye, were hundreds of snares, quick-acting, strong enough to pierce flesh and cause a child to bleed to death quickly. Jenny felt sick, faint.

"Pamela didn't take the time to look in on her this morning," he said, his voice bitter. "She was in a hurry to get out of here—she planned to just take off and leave Judy."

"But—the driver said they both—"

"He *thought* Judy went with her mother. It wasn't until I found out they were both gone that I put it together. Pam went to the airport all right, but she didn't take Judy with her!"

"Damien, I'll do anything I can to help; you know that."

He closed his eyes for a second. "Call Paul Du Mond and tell him I need him to help search. Tell him to bring anybody he can find!"

He was gone then; she had a thousand questions to ask,

but there was no time. She had begun to shake, to tremble, only slightly at first, and then harder, until finally she realized she was either going to have to grab hold of something or else she would faint. The agony and guilt in his eyes had been like sorrowful windows to his soul; Jenny had a quick glimpse into them and she would never again be able to tell herself he meant nothing to her. From this moment on, no matter what, she would love him with certainty, and if she could prove that to him, she would, gladly.

It was Maggie who managed, coolly and calmly, to get the entire story from Jenny and then relate it to the others, speaking Swahili. Then, with the help of Manguana, small groups of people were organized to do various things—the men and boys, of course, were all out searching the bush, but inside, there was food to be prepared, coffee to make, and, of course, all the time they were doing those things, silent prayers to be said.

There had been, Jenny knew, much valuable time lost. From the time Damien and the others began searching the heavily vegetated bush to the time darkness fell was only a matter of hours. Little Judith Anne had been out there somewhere not only the entire day, but perhaps the night as well, or at least a part of it. She had run away sometime in the night, without ever going to bed.

The question was, why hadn't her parents looked in on her, to say goodnight or to kiss her goodnight? Her mother hadn't even bothered to say goodbye to her when she left for London.

But there was no use blaming Damien now, not for anything. From time to time, he would come back to the house in his truck, his eyes holding a muted kind of agony. Was there any word? Did anyone bring the maps he had ordered? He stood in the kitchen, very tall and big, looking down at the maps they brought to him, and, surrounded by whatever men were there, he mapped out territories to be covered. Two of the men ran into snares; they were briefly treated in Maggie's kitchen by Manguana, who remained stoic, silent, and a rock for everyone. Most of the children who lived on the reserve huddled in the kitchen, under the big preparing table or near Manguana's old wood stove. They knew; their frightened eyes said they knew.

Nothing Jenny could have said to them, no posters she could have painted, no words she could have asked to have translated so that they would understand, could possibly have had the impact this was having on them in regard to poaching. There was, they had been told gently by Manguana, a child out there, the little American girl who had come to visit. She was out there somewhere, and they must all pray that she did not become entangled in one of the traps set by their fathers or uncles or older brothers.

From time to time, Jenny would go to the porch. Most of the time, she worked close to Manguana, helping to peel potatoes for the hot meal that was being served to any and all as they filed into the kitchen. Then, either Maggie or Jenny would serve the weary men who came in, handing them iced glasses containing a tea made from the herbs Manguana carried in a small pouch around her fat waist.

It was dark when Heller and Paul Du Mond came in. Heller came straight to Jenny, her face anxious.

"We just got back from Mombas. Paul's giving lectures there twice a week. A friend of Manguana's met our plane and told us about Judy." She shook her head worriedly, openly upset. "Judy Anne was always a spunky kid; never did like her mother very much and who can blame her? Somebody should have checked on her!" She was pacing the floor. Paul had already hopped into one of the jeeps out in front, taking off for the bush with five other men who'd been out there for hours. "I know," she said, gentling a bit, "how Damien feels about his daughter, how he *really* feels." She looked at Jennifer with steady eyes. "I think," she said softly, "it's important for you to understand that about him, Jenny. I also happen to feel that it's important for you to stay with him, no matter what happens."

Jenny's face was moist from the steam in the large room. She went to the back door and at once, a small, warm breeze touched her face.

"I don't understand him, Heller. I don't think I ever will."

"He lost his son and he can't pull himself out of the depths; it's that simple. Paul and I have known that all along—we waited, at first, because to medical people, death is so common that you build a fence around your feelings. We thought Damien would grieve, but he was always very strong, very tough-minded, very dedicated, you see, so we thought in a matter of months or even weeks, he'd be fine again. Maybe if Pamela had been a real wife to him—but she wasn't, not ever, and I suppose that was why his children always meant so much to him."

Jenny turned from the door. "He was cold to Judy. She—she told me he didn't want her." Tears of frustration filled her eyes. "Heller, if Damien had only gone in to kiss Judy goodnight, he'd have seen that her bed was empty and a search party could have been sent out last night, barely twenty-four hours ago." She took a shaking breath. "That," she said, "is what I can't understand!"

She wanted to hate him; she really did. It would be easier. Hate him instead of feeling the way she did about him, despise him instead of seeing the agony in his eyes and wanting to stop it. If she could only convince herself that the agony was deserved; that he had failed his little girl and now he was paying for that failure to love and want the child.

But she could not hate him. She could not.

"Jenny dear," Heller said quietly. "Damien's loss, when Robbie died, was far greater than any of us realized. His future was wrapped up in his kids. He brought them here, and when his son died so soon after they got here, Damien blamed himself. After a while, Paul and I talked about it, when we realized he'd gone into some kind of cocoon. We understood that he would have to either come out of it more dedicated than ever to medicine, to this country and its people, or else he'd go the other way."

"And he went the other way. Totally."

"Yes," Heller said. "He put on a mask and became a kind of—of rich overseer, a man who deals with dollars and cents, nothing to get emotional about. Jenny, the reason he didn't want his daughter to stay here, the reason he didn't go to her room to kiss her and behave like a loving father, has nothing to do with his feeling for her. Or maybe it has everything to do with it. He didn't want to love her so much that he couldn't bear to have her leave him. So he tried not to love her at all." Heller came over to the screened-in door where Jenny stood. She put her hand on Jenny's shoulder. "He did that with you, too, you know."

Jenny closed her eyes, trying hard not to break down. She must not; she must not.

"If Judy dies, Heller, what will happen to him?"

"I don't know," Heller said softly. "But whatever happens, please, please be there with him!"

Jenny nodded. Another truck had pulled up in front, filled with men who had been searching the bush, calling, hacking away at the thick undergrowth with sharp machetes. She went at once to the food table and began filling plates. One of the men came up to her, his kind face haggard with worry.

"Don't think we'll find her. We found many snares, but didn't find the child. Some think maybe something came and found her caught and—"

Jenny's heart seemed to stop. "Some animal found her, you mean? Found her and—"

"Animals don't tell no difference between an elk in a snare and a child in a snare. They got to eat."

"Oh my God." Jenny went out on the porch and leaned

against the post. She looked beyond, at the dark lake and somehow, its peaceful tranquility gave her hope. *Please, Lord, don't let that happen to Damien's child. Spare her; give her back to him—You know how much he has already suffered!*

It was nearly midnight when the message came for Damien. Jennifer hadn't seen him for hours. He had come in to drink tea and check to see if there was any news, and he had briefly glanced at Jennifer. In that moment, she saw his eyes—they were veiled, hardened. It was as if she meant nothing at all to him.

Shortly before he folded up the maps and started to go back out to his truck, the boy came in, breathless. He spoke first to Manguana, then to Damien, in a trembling little voice. Manguana bent over him kindly, listening; when she straightened up, she looked hard at Damien, but said nothing.

Damien answered, speaking quietly but firmly; Jenny couldn't understand any of what he said except for the name, *Dr. Du Mond*. He shook his head, pointing to the darkness outside.

"I have to leave," he said finally.

Jenny came a bit closer to him. "Is there news?"

"No. Nothing about my daughter. The boy came to tell us a child is sick in the village." He looked at Jenny; it was as if a fire blazed in his eyes. "If they find my daughter and she is dead, leave her here, please. I'll take her to Nairobi myself."

"Yes," Jenny said, her voice surprisingly steady. "Damien, let me come with you, please—"

But he was gone, out the door into the black, threatening night.

TWELVE

Only Maggie and the stoic Manguana seemed sane that night, as the carloads and truckloads of men increased, as more heard the news of the white man's lost child and came to help. Only a very few spoke English; between her kitchen duties Manguana patiently translated. The children refused to go to bed; they slept on the floor, huddled close to each other. Some crept under the big kitchen table and some brought their little grass mats and lay down on the porch, eyes wide and frightened.

Jennifer tried not to think of the little girl out there. She tried very hard to think of the child here, brought back safely, hugged, kissed, loved. She tried to picture Damien's eyes when he knew Judith Anne was safe.

But it was hard; the cruel snares with the deadly loop of wire that caught a neck or a leg in it so easily kept sliding into her mind. When an animal became caught in the woven strands of the steel wire, the frenzied struggle to escape only sank the noose deeper into its flesh.

She could not bear such thoughts. Whenever they crowded in on her, Jenny went to Maggie's side, pretending to be busy bringing coffee or hot tea or whatever was being served. Or she stood silently next to Manguana in the kitchen, washing dishes, cups, and pans, gaining strength from doing the mundane things.

Nobody cried, not even the children. Death was nothing new to them; they had all seen animals gravely hurt and suffering, caught in the pliable yet unstretchable and unbreakable snares. Unlike a hunter with a gun or a spear, the deadly snare did not distinguish between young or

183

old—or even between species. They could kill a child as easily as they killed animals.

The search went on; sometime before dawn, Jennifer saw the big searchlights mounted on trucks that had been brought all the way from Nairobi. They flashed like comets in the dark jungle beyond Maggie's house.

"You'd better get off your feet awhile," Heller told Jenny some time before morning. "You don't want to pass out on us, you know."

"I'm fine," Jenny told her.

"You aren't fine. Look, I'm a nurse, remember? Now come and sit down and have a cup of tea. We're just spinning our wheels in here anyway, waiting. We've got enough food ready to feed all of Africa, I'd say. Come on, Jenny, there's a nice, obedient girl."

They sat in the kitchen at Manguana's big table, which groaned with food she'd cooked all night. Outside there was the sound of an occasional vehicle starting up, but other than that, silence. Maggie had gone upstairs to sleep for a few hours.

"What will happen to Damien if they find Judy dead, Heller? Will he be able to survive, do you think?"

Heller had put the tea kettle on. Now she sat across from Jenny at the end of the table, her face calm. There was a certain serenity about Heller that was enchanting; one felt that throughout any kind of crisis, she would remain the same: calm, capable and good-natured. No wonder her husband seemed so much in love with her!

"I don't ever predict what will happen to people under terrible pressure because there's always the human spirit to deal with," Heller said, "and that's an unknown quantity. Sometimes what we think we hate we will eventually come to love—or at least respect." She began buttering some of Manguana's bread for them both. "I came here because Paul and Damien had a dream," she said quietly. "I hated it here. I refused to give my husband a child here. I grew

184

orchids and babied them instead. I refused to get involved in the running feud between your aunt and people like her, and Damien with his ideas about survival of the fittest. Then, I suppose I began to change, from inside out. It's hard to live here and stand back and refuse to get involved."

"Do you mean you're actually happy here?"

"I suppose I am, in a strange way. I know that poaching is deadly and wrong, but I'm not so sure that locking animals up, so to speak, the way Maggie and all of you do, is the right answer. Paul thinks the future of Africa lies in game ranching, Jenny. Animals are controlled by slaughtering them to sell, just as farmers do cattle. Or farmers let people come onto their property to take pictures or to hunt game, for a price. That way, the people eat, the forests don't get chewed away because of animal overpopulation, and the animals survive as a species. It's very likely the only way out of what's been happening here."

"Then, teaching the children about farming, getting them acquainted with this kind of life style—"

"Exactly. If it works, it would do away with poaching forever."

Jenny looked out the window to the breaking dawn. *God, let Damien's child be safe this day! Bring her back to us—her father needs her so!*

She thought there had been a breakthrough when she heard the truck roar up. It was nearly seven; the day was going to be moist and hot. Already some of the men had taken time out to sleep; they lay about the grass in front, catching perhaps thirty minutes of sleep before going back out into the bush to search.

It was Damien's truck; he jumped out and hurried quickly up the porch steps, striding toward the kitchen where Heller and Jenny and Manguana were preparing breakfast for the children.

185

She saw at once that he looked terrible, like a man in a nightmare. His voice was low and controlled, but his eyes held agony. He needed a shave and he looked exhausted.

"Anything?"

"Nothing yet," Heller said stoutly. "Come and eat, Damien. Now that it's light, it will be much easier to find her."

"Is everybody out now?"

"Most of them," Heller said, pouring coffee for him. "How's the baby?"

"Pneumonia. He'll be all right; I left medicine. Where's Paul?"

"Out on one of the trucks, I think." Heller glanced at Jenny. "I'm going to check and see if he needs a lunch sent out there for everybody. Excuse me."

So Jenny found herself alone with him. She put the dish of coarsely ground sugar in front of his cup and then busied herself with the frying eggs.

"Jennifer?"

She did not turn around. There was a certain depth, a quality to his voice that she had not heard before.

"Yes, Damien?"

"I'm going to go back into medicine. When we find my daughter, one way or the other, I'm going to talk to Paul about it." She turned to look at him; he shook his head like a wounded fighter. "I've been dead ever since I lost my son. If I'd reacted differently, with the attitudes that these people have about death, my daughter wouldn't be out there now. She wouldn't have felt that nobody wanted her." His eyes closed. He was, Jenny saw, weeping, weeping silently, trying not to, unable not to. "I didn't hold her; I didn't tell her I cared for her, that I had missed her every moment of every day, because I was afraid to keep her here, afraid for her to stay here. If only I'd held her in my arms and told her how much I love her—"

His head dropped to his folded arms. The wide shoulders

186

suddenly shuddered, although he made no sound. Jennifer watched him for a few heartbeats, then she went to his side, kneeling next to him, reaching out with her arms to hold him.

She held him as she would a child, with her arms tight around him. His face was buried in her soft hair; he made no sounds as he wept, but she felt the wetness from his weeping moisten her hair. Her gentle hands touched his face as she murmured to him, trying to give him hope, telling him it wasn't finished, wasn't over, that a new day had dawned and surely, surely this day they would find Judy—

Suddenly, he moved in her arms and looked at her. His blue eyes were bloodshot from worry and fatigue; there were tears swimming in them.

"I love you," he said, very quietly, not moving. "I want you to know that."

She put her cool cheek against his. And from that moment on, from the essence of herself, from the depths of her spirit, she dedicated herself to making this man happy, to being a comfort and a friend to him, to loving him now and forever, no matter what.

That was the way Maggie found them when she burst into the room, wearing her long white nightgown, her feet bare, a look of excitement in her eyes.

"Something has happened! From upstairs, from my window, I saw two of the jeeps coming down the road, coming fast! Surely they wouldn't drive that way unless—"

Damien jumped up. "Get the food off this table immediately. Spread newspapers on it and get everybody out of the kitchen and keep them out!"

But there was, Jenny saw moments later, no need for any of that.

The jeep pulled up in front, after having stopped to pick up Damien, who had run down the road to meet it, his medical bag in one hand. The women waited on the porch; Jennifer's hand reached for her aunt's and she held on very tightly.

Damien was in the back with his child on his lap; he had his arms around her. Jenny held her breath, hoping against hope, as he got out, carrying little Judy in his arms. There was a hush; not a person made a sound as he proceeded toward the porch.

"Stand by to assist me treat some mild scratches, Heller," Damien said, and then a sudden roar went up from the crowd gathered around and Jennifer saw that the child moved in her father's arms. Judy's face was pressed against his chest.

Fifteen minutes later, Damien came around the back of the house, to where Jennifer stood on the porch.

"I want to thank you," he said quietly. "You saved Judy's life. If she hadn't heard you talking to the kids about the snares, she never would have stayed put, waiting for us to find her, instead of wandering around looking for us."

"We all prayed for her," Jenny said. And then, because she knew that was what he wanted, she went into his arms. They stood very still, close. Finally, he gently raised her face with one hand, so that she was looking into his eyes.

"My daughter and I need you, Jenny."

She smiled, wise as all loved women are wise.

"I know that," she said. And she raised her face for his kiss.

Bestsellers

☐ **COMES THE BLIND FURY** by John Saul $2.75 (11428-4)
☐ **CLASS REUNION** by Rona Jaffe $2.75 (11408-X)
☐ **THE EXILES** by William Stuart Long $2.75 (12369-0)
☐ **THE BRONX ZOO** by Sparky Lyle and
   Peter Golenbock $2.50 (10764-4)
☐ **THE PASSING BELLS** by Phillip Rock $2.75 (16837-6)
☐ **TO LOVE AGAIN** by Danielle Steel $2.50 (18631-5)
☐ **SECOND GENERATION** by Howard Fast $2.75 (17892-4)
☐ **EVERGREEN** by Belva Plain $2.75 (13294-0)
☐ **CALIFORNIA WOMAN** by Daniel Knapp $2.50 (11035-1)
☐ **DAWN WIND** by Christina Savage $2.50 (11792-5)
☐ **REGINA'S SONG**
   by Sharleen Cooper Cohen $2.50 (17414-7)
☐ **SABRINA** by Madeleine A. Polland $2.50 (17633-6)
☐ **THE ADMIRAL'S DAUGHTER**
   by Victoria Fyodorova and Haskel Frankel $2.50 (10366-5)
☐ **THE LAST DECATHLON** by John Redgate $2.50 (14643-7)
☐ **THE PETROGRAD CONSIGNMENT**
   by Owen Sela $2.50 (16885-6)
☐ **EXCALIBUR!** by Gil Kane and John Jakes $2.50 (12291-0)
☐ **SHOGUN** by James Clavell $2.95 (17800-2)
☐ **MY MOTHER, MY SELF** by Nancy Friday $2.50 (15663-7)
☐ **THE IMMIGRANTS** by Howard Fast $2.75 (14175-3)

At your local bookstore or use this handy coupon for ordering:

Dell **DELL BOOKS**
P.O. BOX 1000, PINEBROOK, N.J. 07058

Please send me the books I have checked above. I am enclosing $_____
(please add 75¢ per copy to cover postage and handling). Send check or money
order—no cash or C.O.D.'s. Please allow up to 8 weeks for shipment.

Mr/Mrs/Miss_____

Address_____

City_____State/Zip_____

Love—the way you want it!

Candlelight Romances

MADELEINE A. POLLAND

SABRINA

Beautiful Sabrina was only 15 when her blue eyes first met the dark, dashing gaze of Gerrard Moynihan and she fell madly in love—unaware that she was already promised to the church.

As the Great War and the struggle for independence convulsed all Ireland, Sabrina also did battle. She rose from crushing defeat to shatter the iron bonds of tradition . . . to leap the convent walls and seize love—triumphant, enduring love—in a world that could never be the same.

A Dell Book $2.50 (17633-6)

At your local bookstore or use this handy coupon for ordering: